FIREBALL

FIREBALL

Their identities are hidden in anonymity.
They are the élite, the daring loners of the
sea. They are the men of the Special Boat
Squadron. Plucked from the midst of the
Falklands conflict, SBS Team Alpha are
ordered into an area dominated by the
combined fleets of the Warsaw Pact. Their
mission is to retrieve parts of a Soviet
experimental satellite, the Fireball, before
its masters can mount a recovery operation,
but the crack Russian paratroops, The Red
Eagles, are already en route to the
splashdown zone, and the Fireball will not
be lost without a fight.

FIREBALL

by

John Kerrigan

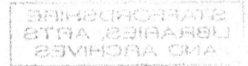

Dales Large Print Books
Long Preston, North Yorkshire,
BD23 4ND, England.

British Library Cataloguing in Publication Data.

Kerrigan, John
    Fireball.

A catalogue record of this book is
available from the British Library

ISBN   978-1-84262-770-9 pbk

First published in Great Britain in 1983 by Jonathan Cape

Cover illustration © Nic Skerten by arrangement with
Arcangel Images

Published in Large Print 2010 by arrangement with
Mrs Gillian Tidmus-Whiting

Dales Large Print is an imprint of Library Magna Books Ltd.

Printed and bound in Great Britain by
T.J. (International) Ltd., Cornwall, PL28 8RW

INTRODUCTION

The Special Boat Squadron

Forty years ago now, run-down Greek *caiques* and flimsy canvas canoes flitted in and out of the remoter inlets of the Aegean and Mediterranean, bearing bold, bronzed men of a half a dozen Allied nations. These men, all volunteers who had messed about in boats in civilian life, fought private little battles with the Germans, the Italians and their various Balkan Allies, in a war which has remained secret to this very day. They raised the locals in fierce clandestine warfare, in which no quarter was given or expected; they sabotaged railways and petrol drums; they kidnapped high-ranking German generals and blackmailed Italian ones into surrender. They were the SAS of the sea – the brave loners of the SPECIAL BOAT SQUADRON.

In 1945, the men of the SBS were officially disbanded and returned to civilian life, to spend their weekends mucking about in boats again. But *did* they?

For if so, who were the men in the non-descript uniforms, armed with weapons manufactured in half a dozen non-aligned countries, who fought so bitterly against the Army of Indonesia in Borneo? Who were those hit-and-run fighters who were the terror of the Communist-inspired guerrillas on the long coastline of the Gulf of Aden? Who were those anonymous troops who landed on the Falklands long before the Task Force ever went into action?

The 'minders', those much-hated bowler-hatted civilians from the Ministry of Defence who censored the cables of the journalists attached to the Falklands Task Force, managed to keep out of the dispatches all reference to the mysterious seaborne troops who went in first. Yet one little clue to the identity of those clandestine raiders did slip through without the 'minders' knowing. It was contained in a rather crude cartoon by Warrant Officer Roy Carr of the Royal Marines, which appeared in a collection published to aid the South Atlantic Fund. It showed a burly Marine surrounded by three penguins, shouting back to his superior officer: *'Apparently they're SBS and have been here three weeks already... Oh, and sir, they want to know if we've got any fish!'*

SBS. In other words, those mysterious raiders of the South Atlantic belonged to an organization which was supposed to have been disbanded these forty years. This, then, is their story. The story of the men who steal from the sea to fight and to win, and who disappear into the mists as mysteriously as they came. It is the story of the élite of the élite: THE SPECIAL BOAT SQUADRON...

BOOK ONE

Falklands To Finland

'So those of you who live to talk,
Let your pride hover as does the hawk
And never let men these acts forget.'

Ode to Tumbledown
Anonymous Scots Guardsman,
June 1982

I

An icy wind hissed down the loch, bringing with it cold showers of thin, grey rain. Dull-white spurts of spray rippled the surface of the water and rocked the black, sinister shape of the submarine anchored there. Overhead, the sky was as bleak and forbidding as the sea; the only sound was the wild screeching of the seagulls searching for scraps of food in this remote, inhospitable place.

'Did yer know, mate, there's ten thousand frigging sheep in the place to every frigging kelper?' snarled a harsh Scouse voice. 'God only knows what the frigging Argies see in the friggin place! Frigging arsehole of the world!'

Lieutenant Roger Mallory, Royal Marines, grinned as he fastened the heavy bottles to his wet suit. The disgruntled Liverpudlian was right. South Georgia really was the end. Still, this remote island promised to be the scene of his first taste of active service after five long years of training. Even Marine Rogers, eighteen years old and the youngest of his team, was excited at the prospect, asking him over and over again on the way out whether there'd be a gong in it. In the end,

Sergeant Ross had silenced him with that iron-hard Gorbals look of his, and a curt, 'Yer, a putty one – and I'll shove it up yer arse, laddie, if yer dinna stop yer chatter!'

Mallory tapped the catches, his good-humoured, handsome face set in a frown of concentration; then he pulled on his black rubber hood. He watched as his team readied themselves on the dripping deck of the little hunter-sub which had brought them eight thousand miles to this remote place to carry out their secret mission, so vital to the success of the Task Force still a thousand miles or more away on the South Atlantic.

They were a mixed bunch, but tough and reliable, each man a specialist in his own field. Ross, the sergeant – bitter, twisted, resentful, the typical product of a slum childhood in the Gorbals, yet as hard as nails and as brave as they came. Corporal Ramsbottom, known behind his back as 'Sheepsarse' – a big, bluff Yorkshireman, completely unflappable. Rifleman Bin Bahadur, seconded from the Gurkhas – skinny and seemingly frail, but possessing more stamina and staying-power than the rest of them put together. And finally the baby of the team, Rogers, eighteen months in the Marines and as 'randy as a bluidy goat', to quote the words of Sergeant Ross. 'All yon man thinks on is slipping it in some poxed-up bint!' Yet in spite of his low IQ and deplorable ambition to

14

service every loose woman in Pompey, Mallory was ready to admit that the lad was nothing if not willing. He was also an undoubted genius with his hands and seemed to be able to tackle any kind of electronic gadgetry. 'Ay, that he can,' Ross had admitted sourly more than once to Mallory. 'It comes, ye ken, sir, from fiddling around with the spare parts o' all them loose women!'

On the bridge, the skipper of the sub looked down at Mallory's team apprehensively before flinging another glance at the leaden, threatening sky. Mallory knew why. It wasn't the rain that the skipper was worried about; it was the Argy Sky Hawks. He gave the matelot one of his crooked, knowing smiles and raised his right thumb to signify that they were ready. With obvious relief, the skipper returned the signal and prepared to dive, rapping out quick, urgent commands. Above, the seagulls shrieked angrily, as if they knew they would be soon deprived of their scraps.

Mallory flashed his team a last look. They were all ready, faces suddenly tense at the thought of what lay ahead of them. Even Sergeant Ross's red, brooding face revealed some of his inner tension. Like Mallory, he had trained for years for this moment. But that had been training; this was the real thing at last.

Mallory swallowed and tried to steady

himself. 'Just butterflies,' he muttered to himself, aping Rifleman Bahadur's pronunciation of the word, 'just butterflies'. 'All right, chaps,' he barked, 'here we go! Good luck – and good hunting!' Next moment he flipped himself backwards over the side of the sub, whose engines were already beginning to purr as it prepared to dive.

Swiftly, one by one, the rest of the SBS team did the same. One moment they were there, the next they were gone. A splash, a burst of white water, a flurry of bubbles; then nothing – just the heaving grey-green of the loch.

'Frigging heroes, the frigging lot of 'em,' the scouse voice commented, as the bells jingled softly and the beat of the sub's engines grew ever louder. 'Wouldn't have their frigging job for all the frigging tea in China, Chalkey!'

'What d' yer expect?' his oppo remarked unfeelingly. 'Marines, ain't they?' he added, as if that were explanation enough. 'That's what they get paid for. Dead keen, that SBS lot. Enjoy it, they do, fiddling around underwater in enemy territory. Probably get more fun out of that than getting it in the old pearly gates of a pay-night.' He dismissed the frogmen. 'Come on, Scouse, the cooks have got them thin beef bangers for breakfast. Let's get 'em before them greedy sods of the first watch nab 'em all...'

Five minutes later, the submarine had vanished and the loch was empty again. Lieutenant Mallory and his team were on their own now.

Mallory swam easily, effortlessly, hardly aware he was doing so, breathing steadily and slowly, filling and emptying his lungs at regular, controlled intervals, aware that he must not use up the 'mix' too rapidly. The team would need reserves – just in case.

Now the light was greenish as it filtered down from above. Little bits of suspended matter barred his way here and there. A couple of times he saw the silver flash of big fish, as they fled the approach of these strange, black-clad creatures who gave off a weird, pumping noise unlike any fish they had ever encountered. Occasionally, strings of pearly bubbles escaped from the formation as the five men swam steadily towards their objective, catching and reflecting the light. Mallory knew they would have to watch out for those bubbles once they got closer to shore. The weather up top wasn't very good, but at the briefing in London they had been warned that the Argies had excellent modern surveillance aids – infrared viewers, thermal imagers, image intensifiers, the whole works. He didn't want them to be spotted by some damned Argy marine. That would give the whole bold plan away

17

before they had even started.

He looked at the instruments strapped to his left wrist, next to the wickedly sharp combat knife. He was dead on course, with five minutes swimming time to go. He squirmed round and held up his right hand, the fingers spread to indicate five minutes. The men swimming behind him at five-metre intervals in a loose 'V' nodded acknowledgement.

Mallory swum on, humming a little song. It was one he had learned back in the old days at Gosport when he had first trained for the SBS, with a warning chorus which ran: *'For down at the depth of seventy feet... Lives a guy called Oxygen Pete...'*

Now they were getting close to the shore. Mallory could tell, because the water was becoming darker and dirtier – the effect of the swell breaking on the lonely pebbled beach – the beach that was soon to be the site of the Task Force's first landing and the starting point of the battle to win back the Falkland Islands from the Argies. Mallory could feel the adrenalin begin to pump into his bloodstream. It was a good sign. Physically and mentally he was functioning perfectly, his mind absolutely clear.

Suddenly he almost stopped swimming. He stared hard, as if unable to believe the evidence of his own eyes. Coming towards him was what appeared to be a dead body, swaying gently in the current, glimpsed as if at the bottom of a muddy pool. Then he saw that it was an old overcoat swollen by the water, its empty arms waving grotesquely. Mallory swallowed hard, feeling his heart thumping with shock. Sergeant Ross came level with him. He took in the situation at once and shot Mallory a contemptuous Gorbals look in which was expressed everything he thought about Mallory and the rest of the 'la-di-da upper classes', as he called them. Silently Mallory told Ross to go and fuck himself, and swam on.

Exactly one minute later, just as Intelligence back in London had predicted, they bumped into the first obstacles. There was nothing very sophisticated about them: explosive charges set in pre-cast concrete blocks, surmounted by tripods of steel tubing, from which floated a long, greenish-coloured snag line, almost impossible to detect a few inches below the surface of the water. The idea was that when landing craft passed overhead on their way towards the beach, their propellers would foul the snag line, haul it tight and thus fire the mine.

Mallory turned his thumb down at the first mine and then outwards, left and right. The rest nodded their understanding. They had been trained to tackle much more sophisticated underwater devices than these, but this time it was for real: these mines did not simply contain enough explosive to frighten the unwary or clumsy novice; these would kill a man. And all of them knew, as they spread out and commenced their task, that an underwater blast could kill or maim at incredible distances. A normal depth charge could kill a diver outright at a range of over a mile. However simple the Argy devices were, they couldn't afford to relax their concentration for one second.

Swiftly the team began to fan out, Sergeant Ross to the right, followed by Rogers and Bin Bahadur; Ramsbotham and Mallory to the left, counting the gaps between the tethered mines until they had reached the width of the channel they aimed to clear for the invasion force. Then immediately, without any signal needing to be given – for they had done the job often enough in practice – the two teams turned inwards and began defusing the mines.

Ramsbottom and Mallory worked well together, tackling alternate mines so that not one escaped their scrutiny in the green, dirty water, and flashing each other a blur of a smile as they leap-frogged one another.

Thirty minutes passed ... an hour. Now they had cleared a channel of nearly one hundred metres. But already the tremendous mental strain was beginning to tell. However simple the Argies' system might be, there was always a chance that some cunning regular Argy naval officer, perhaps trained in

20

the UK or the USA, might have booby-trapped it. There was also the risk that the Argies might have their own frogmen patrolling the boom. Worst of all, they might have some electronic surveillance device, unknown to British Intelligence, that could detonate the whole system by remote control – and them with it!

They had now been working flat out for two hours. The channel they had cleared was nearly two hundred metres broad. In another fifteen minutes or so, it would be wide enough for the landing barges. Then, all the Mallory team would have to do would be to swim away to the rendezvous with the sub, leaving the Argies unaware of the fact that their beach defences had been breached. Mallory nodded to Ramsbotham to continue alone, working towards the Ross team, which was already in sight. The big Yorkshire corporal nodded back. Flexing his right shoulder muscle, which was stiff from the strain of twisting and turning the wrench attached by a cord to his right wrist, Mallory swam away to make a quick check on the shallows, just in case the enemy had planted any of his unlovely little devices there.

Almost too late, he saw the twin beams cutting through the green gloom like faint yellow eyes. Malory froze. He knew instinctively it must be the enemy. What kelper would be sea-fishing in weather like this, even if the

Argies had given him permission? Whoever was coming towards him now *had* to be an Argy frogman.

Mallory's brain was racing furiously. He could feel his chest muscles tightening up. In a flash he had begun to breathe too hard and too fast. If he didn't pull himself together in a minute, he would start hyperventilating. He would begin to tremble, feel giddy and panic. *'Cool it, Roger,'* he told himself, and forced himself to breathe more slowly. His eyes narrowed to slits as he attempted to pierce the gloom of the shallows.

Now a black, rippling shape was just visible behind the lamp. The unknown Argy was moving slowly, pushing the twin beams in front of him as if he had all the time in the world. From the leisurely way he swam, Mallory guessed the enemy suspected nothing. To him, this was probably just a routine inspection of the underwater defences, a boring task which he carried out casually, not suspecting that the English enemies were not a couple of thousand kilometers away, as he had been told by his officers, but right here, only metres from him.

Slowly, deliberately, with a conscious effort of will, Mallory began to draw his knife from the sheath on his other wrist. He could now see that the lone frogman had only one bottle of compressed air on his back. That made him perhaps thirty pounds lighter than himself. Furthermore, the enemy hadn't had a thirty minute swim behind him and another ninety minutes of hard physical labour defusing the mines. The advantage was definitely on the other man's side.

For some reason the words of a long-forgotten lecture at training school on the hazards of diving in tropical waters came back to Mallory at that moment. 'The octopus is a timid but curious creature,' explained the grey-haired old instructor, who had worn the ribbons of the Old War on his chest. 'But when it's disturbed, it'll get frightened and bring its tentacles into play. The thing to do is to get as close to its body as possible. Some people say that the octopus is very sensitive where the tentacles join the body, and that you should try to tickle it under the armpits, whereupon it'll convulse itself with laughter.' The old instructor's voice hardened. 'Personally,' he rasped, 'I don't believe a word of it. For my money, the best method is to go in for the kill – *and stab the bugger right in the eye with yer knife!*' And with that he had thrust out his hand and given a vivid demonstration. The move had caught Mallory off guard, and even now he recalled almost falling off his chair in surprise.

Now he realized with an awful feeling of trepidation that he was being expected to do just that – 'stab the bugger right in the eye.'

The lone frogman was only metres away. Fortunately for Mallory, paddling there in the green shallows, he was concentrating on the beams and looking neither to left nor right. Otherwise he would have spotted the SBS man long ago. Mallory knew now that he had to kill him – there was no alternative. The enemy frogman could not live to tell what he would soon see. That would endanger the success of the entire landing. For the first time in his young life – a life based on the security and assurance of inherited wealth, good breeding and the honour of belonging to a Corps in which his family had served for at least five generations – Roger Mallory prepared to kill someone. It would not be the last time.

In seconds the Argy would see him. Now Mallory made a quick assessment of the situation. Speed would be on the other fellow's side; surprise on his.

Then it happened. The twin beams were directed straight at him. Mallory didn't wait for the other man's gasp of surprise. He dived up and forwards, kicking out hard with his flippers. The beams fell from the Argy's grasp, and in that same instant Mallory dropped on him, knife gripped firmly in one hand, his other hand feeling for the feller's mask.

With surprising suddenness the Argy reacted. He did a kind of underwater somersault. Mallory missed him by inches. He caught a fleeting glimpse of a scared, swarthy face behind the round circle of glass, then the Argy was kicking out for the bottom. Mallory dived after him, the twin beams staring up at him from the seabed like jaundiced, accusing eyes.

The Argy hit the bottom. Desperately he struggled with his tank, clearly intending to ditch it and race to the surface. Mallory knew he couldn't allow him to do that; they couldn't be more than fifty yards from the beach. With all his strength he kicked out. The Argy forgot the tank. His knee came up, and Mallory gasped as it caught him in the crotch. The water cushioned the cruel blow a little, but even so he nearly vomited into his mask with the shock. The knife went reeling from his nerveless fingers.

A flurry of bubbles from the Argy's mask alerted Mallory to his danger. He tensed himself. Just in time. The Argy's knife flashed. Up went Mallory's right arm, parrying the blow at the very last moment. Now he forgot his pain and his weariness. His hand shot forward, searching for the other man's mask clips.

Frantically the Argy wriggled, trying to hold his face out of reach. But Mallory's reach was longer. He found the clips. He grunted and pulled hard. Suddenly bubbles were shooting wildly for the surface, and there was a sinister hiss of compressed air escaping.

The Argy, his mouth gaping open like a stranded fish, tried to thrust Mallory to one side. To no avail. Desperately Mallory held on to the side of his rubber hood, while the other man kicked and thrashed in panic. Now bubbles were exploding in one long, continuous stream from his gasping, gaping mouth. He began to make furious little strangled sounds. Mallory watched almost clinically as the other man's face began to change colour, turning slowly but inevitably to that pink that indicated approaching death, his dark eyes rolling wildly, seeming to bulge out of his head as he drowned, held there in that cruel, unyielding grip.

With one last tug, the dying Argy attempted to break loose, while Mallory held on for grim death, sobbing with effort, the sweat streaming down his taut body, his nerves tingling electrically. But the Argy hadn't a chance. Mallory was stronger. Jaw jutting, muscles aflame with the strain, he applied that last killing pressure, and suddenly the Argy frogman went limp in his hands.

But still Mallory wasn't taking any chances. He held on a little longer, cradling the man in his arms as if they were lovers, forcing himself to count off the seconds until two minutes had passed. Then, and only then, did he relax his grip and gaze down at the man he had just murdered.

His face was turning from pink to a ghastly greyish-purple colour, the saliva drooling from his slack, crimson lips. From his mouth-piece came obscure bubbling noises.

He had killed a man. He would never be the same again. Mallory shook his head, as if attempting to wake from a bad dream. But it wasn't a bad dream; it was reality. He had killed a man.

With the last of his strength, Mallory seized the back of the dead Argy's hood and started back the way he had come, towing the dead Argy after him, like a weary fisherman bringing home his catch after a long, hard struggle...

2

Down in the hangar they were showing video porn. Miss Lovelace was about to open that marvelous mouth of hers again, and the marines and matelots were clutching their third can of rationed *Long Life* in palms that were wet and sticky with sweat. Up top, it was red alert, and the Harrier pilots already sat in their cockpits, waiting for the Mirages to come zooming in.

For his part, Lieutenant Mallory lay

slumped on his bunk, alternating between the *Economist* and *Penthouse,* sipping his *Chivas Regal* and wondering which of the two publications told the best lies. It was forty-eight hours now since the successful landing, and he was bored, waiting for another assignment for his team. His men were, too. The sight of him towing back the dead enemy frogman had shocked them. Even underwater, he had been able to see that. But once back on board the aircraft carrier, they had recovered soon enough. Since then, they had seen several other 'stiffs', and like all soldiers in all wars were becoming tough, unfeeling and not a little brutalized by combat. Now they craved action again.

'Can ye no sweet-talk the Admiral into giving us another job o' work on yon big island?' Sergeant Ross had snarled. 'With all this damn porn they keep showing, the lads are wanking themselves stupid. Getting soft, they are. Even yon black feller Bahadur's stopped sharpening that kukri thing o' his! Another week o' this and them soft nellies won't be able to fight their way out of a paper bag, *sir!*'

Mallory had sighed. It irked him to find himself in agreement with Sergeant Ross, but this time he was right. He was bored. They were bored. SBS Team Alpha needed action – and they needed it soon, before this damned war against the Argies was over. He tossed the two mags angrily to one side and kneeling on his bunk, stared hard at the map of the Falklands he had pinned to the bulk-head, trying to guess where the Admiral might need him and his men next.

It was thus that the tall, lean major with the badge of the Intelligence Corps on his cap found him, as he stood there at the door of the little cabin, gazing in. Meanwhile down in the hangar, the matelots and marines could be heard whooping excitedly as Miss Lovelace's velvet throat concluded its amazing performance.

'Saying your prayers, old chap?' he asked.

Mallory turned, startled. The retort he had ready died on his lips at the sight of the superior officer with the red band of the staff around his cap. He sprang to attention.

'No, sir, just looking at the map. Wonder-ing where they might be assigning me and my chaps next.'

Up top, the alarm sirens began to shrill. The Mirages were coming again, and there was a thunder of jet engines as the Harriers began to take off to meet the challenge. Suddenly the corridor outside seemed to be full of matelots in flash gear and helmets, running in all directions. In an instant all seemed controlled confusion.

But the new alert left the strange major seemingly unmoved. He continued to stare at Mallory, as if trying to imprint his every feature on his memory, oblivious to the noise and the jeers of the video watchers as the screen went dead and Miss Lovelace's cunning lips and wonderfully accommodating velvet throat disappeared for the night. In a minute the disgruntled matelots would be throwing their empty beer cans at the screen.

The major smiled, but his smart, searching eyes did not light up. 'Well, I shall tell you something for free, Lieutenant Mallory, your next assignment will *not* be in the Falklands. You and your chaps are going home toot sweet – very toot sweet indeed.'

Mallory gasped. 'What did you say, sir?' he stuttered, taken aback. What emergency could possibly have arisen to necessitate such an urgent recall?

The intelligence officer did not answer his question. 'Sorry, Mallory. I should have introduced myself. I'm Richardson – Intelligence Signals, you know.'

Mallory didn't know. He had never heard of such a unit. Somehow he suspected Major Richardson wasn't all he was supposed to be. On the surface, he looked like one of those clean-cut jocks that one came across so often in the service these days – men who could snatch-lift two hundred pounds and jogged twenty miles before breakfast. In reality, he probably had a Double First in

Slavonic languages and computer science from Cambridge and read Günter Grass in the original over port in the evening. A cunning bugger, in other words.

'I'm your escorting officer, you see, Mallory.'

'Escorting officer,' Mallory repeated in a daze. 'Escorting ... where?'

Up above, the guns were beginning to pound. The Harriers had now cleared the decks and the Mirages were zooming in for the attack.

'First out of this rather – er – dangerous place,' Richardson replied, 'and on to a very fast frigate which will take you to Ascension. From there we fly.'

'Frigate ... Ascension?' Mallory stuttered. The carrier heaved violently, for now the skipper was zig-zagging all out, in an attempt to put the Argy pilots off their aim.

'Yes – at the double, Mallory.' There was iron in the major's voice now. 'You and your chaps have got exactly five minutes. Personal kit only. One hold-all. Weapons – the lot – are to be left behind. You'll be provided with new kit and equipment at your destination. The chopper up there is a sitting duck for the enemy. *Move it!*'

Lieutenant Mallory did just that.

The 30mm cannon blasted tracer shells into the glowing velvet darkness at a thousand rounds a minute. Men were running in all directions. Off the port side of the carrier, a Mirage bellied in the water, burning furiously. The air stank of kerosene. Aft, the medics were hurrying away a Harrier pilot who had crash-landed on the deck, while the fire-fighting teams submerged his wrecked plane in thick, white bubbling foam. All was noise, contained confusion and flames. And now the antiquated Argy Corsairs were coming in again!

Alpha team crowded to the side of the chopper, its blades whirling furiously, waiting for the signal to board, while Major Richardson conferred anxiously with the flight-deck controller. Most of them were awed by the sights all around them, their young faces hollowed out to scarlet death's heads by the flames. Not Sergeant Ross. He loved it.

'Now yon's what I call a real war, laddies!' he yelled above the racket, eyes sparkling fanatically. 'None o' yer nellying about underwater. Real fighting-man's stuff!'

'Ay,' Corporal Ramsbottom commented drily, 'nice kinda war, where a bloke could get his balls shot off right quick and not have so much as a penknife to defend himself.'

Next to him, Rifleman Bahadur waved his kukri. 'Gurkha penknifes bleeding good,' he exclaimed in his fractured English. 'Pity can't fly.'

'All right, Mallory!' Richardson yelled, as a Corsair came screaming in at mast-top height, white rockets hissing from her wings like fiery furious hornets. 'The chopper pilot's going to risk it!'

'At the double, lads!' Mallory bellowed.

'You heard the officer!' Ross snarled. 'Let's be having yer now. At the double!'

Crouched low, bareheaded and carrying their single grips like tourists on a package tour, they raced for the helicopter, whose blades were rotating furiously now as it prepared to take off.

Gasping, they bundled themselves on board, while the crewman, white-helmeted and strapped to the fuselage, kept them covered with the 7.62mm machine-gun. Next moment, amid deafening noise, the chopper was climbing furiously, the crewman swinging the heavy machine-gun to left and right, waiting for the first sight of an enemy plane. Rapidly the carrier started to shrink into the red-glowing gloom of battle below.

'Now that's what I call a right royal send-off!' Mallory yelled into Richardson's ear above the racket of the rotors.

'You ain't seen nothing yet,' Richardson quipped coolly, and pointed through the glass port. 'Look what's coming to see us off!'

'Oh, crikey,' Marine Rogers gasped, 'the bugger's coming straight at us!'

The American-made fighter-bomber, long out of service with most air forces, was indeed hurtling straight towards them, pursued by the lethal white Morse of the tracer shells from the carrier. Soon the naval gunners below would have to cease firing in case they hit the chopper – and the pilot, hunched over his controls up front, knew it. Immediately he tensed and prepared to take evasive action, as the Corsair zipped across the dark sky, heading for them on a crash course.

'*Now!*' he screamed to the gunner over his throat-mike.

The gunner pressed his trigger. The machine-gun burst into frenetic life. A stream of tracer raced towards the Corsair, in the same moment that the chopper pilot threw the machine into a violent left break.

The trick worked. The Argy launched his missiles just a fraction of a second too late, and they hurtled past the wildly bucking chopper like angry express trains. Seconds later, the silver Corsair with the markings of the Argentine Air Force swept above them in a flash of gleaming metal. To Mallory, grimly hanging on inside, it seemed he could have reached out and touched the enemy plane's belly. The mass of silver metal seemed to fill the sky.

It was a target not to be missed. 'Mon,' Ross cursed, 'if I only had yon machine-gun, I'd tear the bugger's guts out of him!'

But the crewman did it for him. Firing at a crazy rate, filling the chopper with the acrid stench of burnt explosive and a mad clatter as the yellow, gleaming cartridge cases tumbled to the deck, the gunner ripped the Corsair to shreds.

'Pilot, he got bottle!' Bahadur cried, yellow face gleaming with excitement, as he swished his razor-sharp kukri through the air. 'Plenty bottle!'

'Watch that bloody penknife, will you!' Marine Rogers yelled in alarm, as the kukri swept down just in front of him. 'Nearly had my goolies off!'

'Arsehole hanging out agen?' Sergeant Ross jeered, as the smoking Corsair came in once again, its pilot obviously carried away by the madness of battle and prepared to sacrifice his own life if only he could bring down the damned British chopper.

But it was not to be. The crewman took deliberate aim. Stricken as it was, with thick, white smoke pouring from its ruptured engine, the Corsair was an easy target. The men of Alpha Team fell silent, gripped by tension, as the crewman led the Argy in – for the kill. Only Mallory was able to speak. 'Out with it, Major,' he cried, as the crew-man's knuckles tensed white over the trigger, 'where are we going?'

The crewman pressed his trigger and the machine-gun burst into frenetic life. The Corsair seemed to stop in mid-air, as if it had just run into a brick wall.

'Finland!' Major Richardson bellowed – and in the same moment, the Corsair disintegrated, setting the chopper off rocking wildly. Suddenly they seemed to be flying through a hail of whirling metal shards, followed by a shattered black thing attached to an open parachute that drifted away into darkness, bearing its dead cargo with it. 'That's where you're bound ... *Finland!'*

'Major Richardson said we were being sent to Finland, sir,' Lieutenant Mallory said to the civilian sitting opposite him in the screened-off first class accommodation of the BEA jet. The stewardess had departed now, leaving them with their drinks, and Mallory felt able to talk more freely. In the background he could already hear the rest of the team shouting for their duty-free allowance. By the time they reached Heathrow they would all be dead drunk. Dismissing them, Mallory turned his attention once more to the middle-aged civilian with the Brigade of Guards tie. In spite of the heat of Ascension Island the man still wore a heavy black pin-striped suit. 'Is that true?'

The civilian trimmed back his clipped

pepper-and-salt moustache with a practiced sweep of his hand and took a sip of his whisky and soda. 'Richardson wasn't authorized to tell you that, Mallory,' he said severely. 'But no matter. You would have found out soon enough.'

'So Finland it is, sir. But why?' Mallory asked a little desperately. 'What would you need the SBS there for?'

The civilian stared hard at Mallory; from the look of him, Mallory guessed that in some previous life he had been a colonel in the Brigade, or something similar.

Colonel Stevens, for his part, took in the younger man's handsome, bronzed, tough face, discounted the somewhat wary and cynical cast of the eyes and noted with pleasure the dimpled chin: a sure sign of a pugnacious nature. 'It's in connection with Fireball – well, that's the NATO code-name for it.'

'Fireball, sir?'

The civilian looked to left and right, almost as if he feared being overheard at twenty thousand feet. 'It's a Soviet experimental laser satellite – a kind of laser gunship floating around in the stratosphere. Everyone's having a crack at them at the moment – the Russians, the Israelis, ourselves naturally, even the Cubans, I believe. You see, if someone *could* come up with a workable laser cannon to be used up there,' he pointed above his head, as if the air above him was filled with whirling satellites, 'then he'd upset the whole applecart. You know – our spy satellites, long-range weather stations, the whole military set-up in the sky.'

Mallory nodded, but inwardly he was more confused than ever. What did all this have to do with him and Alpha?

'Now, Mallory,' the civilian continued, dropping his voice even lower, 'combined NATO Intelligence reports that this Fireball satellite of the Russkis is having some sort of teething troubles and is about to abort. In fact, they've come up with an exact date – really smart johnnies, they are. It's Friday August 13th of this year.'

The civilian took another sip of his whisky. It was as if he could only convey information in small doses – possibly because he felt he was always dealing with people of limited intelligence whom he couldn't burden with too much thinking at any one time.

'Ten years before you were born, Mallory, I was sent to Poland as a very young sub-altern – during the war, of course. By that time we'd heard all about the German experiments with rockets – missiles, as they call them these days – at their testing station on the Baltic at Peenemünde. But we hadn't anything tangible. So when the Polish underground reported that they'd hidden bits and pieces of one of the Boche rockets

– er, *missiles*, in a lake in Western Poland, I was sent to fetch them back to London, you see.'

Again Mallory nodded helplessly, completely bewildered now by the turn the conversation was taking. Back in Economy Class he could hear his team beginning to sing, as the duty-free hooch began to take effect. So far it was relatively harmless: *'Uncle Silvest with all the medals on his chest...'* But it wouldn't stay that way for long. He hoped to God the blonde stewardess wasn't the hysterical type. 'I see, sir,' he said – though he saw nothing.

'Well, I did just that – and it proved of great help to the war effort. In fact, Winston gave me a gong for it, though, of course, it was the Poles who did all the really rough stuff. Poor buggers, the Russkis shot most of them afterwards.' He paused, and tugged at the end of his sharp nose, as if genuinely moved by those long-forgotten tragedies of forty years ago.

'Well, Mallory, we're going to ask you and your chaps to do the same,' he said very suddenly, fixing the young Marine officer with a hard, unwavering stare.

'Do the same, sir?'

'Yes – pick up the bits and pieces of that Russki laser satellite, just as I did long ago. Our backroom boys are simply wetting themselves waiting to get their greedy little

39

paws on the thing.'

'But where, sir? Where am I supposed to pick up the – er – bits and pieces?' Mallory asked, with a trace of desperation.

'The Baltic, Mallory. To be exact off the Baltic coast of *Finland!*'

Back in Economy Class they were singing, *'Big balls, small balls, balls as big as yer head… Give 'em a twist around yer wrist and throw 'em right over yer head…'*

And judging by the high-pitched screams, the blonde stewardess *was* the hysterical type.

3

'Did you know, sir, that the cruiser the *Admiral Scheer* is buried right beneath your feet?' asked the cheerful little German petty officer as the Bundeswehr truck came to a halt and the Alpha team began to drop down to the jetty. 'It was hit by the Royal Air Force–' it was the first time Mallory had ever heard anyone give the RAF their full title '–just at the end of the war. She sank right here. Afterwards, the civic authorities here at Kiel filled in the whole area with rubble from the bombing – including the *Scheer*. So, sir,' he said cheerfully, a broad grin on his plump face, 'you are now walking over the last ship of the Kriegsmarine.'

'Fascinating,' Mallory heard himself say. In fact, it was just another piece of confusing information to add to all the other scraps with which he had been bombarded these last three days. During that time he had been whisked from London to Pompey, from Pompey to Cheltenham, from there to Porterdown, and finally here to Kiel in West Germany – and in each place he had been fed with an amazing mass of details and technicalities by earnest civilians and hard-faced, keen-eyed senior officers, all of them panting to get him started on his mission to recover the damned Fireball.

Once, in exasperation, he had dared to ask the Colonel Commandant, who had known his father and had indeed been his own first CO while he had served with 42 Commando, 'But why us, sir? Why Alpha Team?'

The Colonel Commandant appeared to give the matter serious thought. 'It's not just a case of give Muggins a turn, Roger. It's more than that. The last time the Special Boat Service went into action before this Falklands business was back in Borneo, well over a decade ago. Most of those men have since left the Corps or moved back into one of our more conventional units. You and your chaps of Alpha, Roger, are the only SBS people who've actually seen a shot fired in anger, the only men we've got who've been blooded. That's why you were selected. There's also the fact, Roger, that you are well-known throughout the Corps as being a particularly bloody-minded person when the occasion calls for it,' he added with a tight smile.

Mallory had returned the smile, though he had never felt less like smiling; for by then he had known what was expected of the Alpha Team – and it wasn't good. First, the German Federal Navy would run them deep into the Baltic into an area dominated by the Warsaw Pact's combined fleets. Then they would be landed off the southern coast of Finland, and would complete the rest of the run by kayak under cover of darkness. They would then hide out on that lonely southern Finnish coastline, maintaining constant radio contact with Cheltenham, who would direct them to the area of touch-down on August 13th, making sure that they weren't spotted by the Finns. As the man from MI6 had explained during the briefing in that shabby terrace house in South London, 'The Finns hate the Commies' guts, but they *are* the Russians' nearest neighbours and they're not going to risk any trouble with the Russians on account of you. If they do nab you, Mallory, you'll be lucky if they simply give you the old heave-ho over their frontier with Sweden one dark night. If you're unlucky, they'll make an issue out of it for the sake of the Russkis and you'll land in clink for a year or two. So our advice is not to get nicked...'

'*Not to get nicked...*' The words echoed in the deepest recesses of Mallory's mind as he started to mount the gangway leading to the lean, grey West German torpedo boat. Behind him, Ross was chivvying the men as they unloaded their equipment. '...Come on now! Get them fingers out! Show these Huns just what the Marines can do! Move it!... *And watch them bleeding shooters, will ye, Gunga Din!*' he roared in red-faced fury at Rifleman Bahadur, who was lifting up the small crate containing their WZ 62 machine pistols, the rare Polish-made weapon they would be using on this op. If they had to use force, the slugs would hopefully identify them to the Finnish authorities as members of some Warsaw pact outfit.

Inwardly Mallory winced. Was there any prejudice that Ross did not possess? First 'Huns', and now 'Gunga Din'! That man could start the third world war all on his own.

The elderly Oberleutnant in command of the German ship, who seemed to be very ancient to be of such low rank, took it all in his stride. With German formality, he clicked to attention, touched his hand to his cap – Mallory noticed he wore gloves in spite of the warm weather – and said in faultless English, 'Welcome aboard, Lieutenant Mallory.

Perhaps we should mark the occasion with a verse or two of *"Wir Fahren gegen En-geland"*? We – er, *Huns* sing it all the time. By the way, the name is Maydag.' He saluted again.

Mallory blushed, and Oberleutnant Maydag grinned at his discomfiture...

A stiff wind was blowing across the bay, veering from one northern point to another, making it heavy going for the German torpedo boat. Time and time again she was hit by the wind and was sent yawing violently from side to side.

Mallory braced himself against a stanchion and fought to quell the familiar queasy sensation in his stomach. He would look a damned fool as a sea-going soldier if he got sick in front of Maydag. As for the Oberleutnant, his fat, middle-aged face looked a picture of ruddy health as he watched the young ratings on the bridge and the green-glowing dials of the instruments.

'East Germany,' said Maydag suddenly, and pointed to the dark smudge of land, already beginning to merge into the night. 'That's Wismar light, to be exact.'

Mallory forgot his lurching stomach and stared in the direction indicated, his gaze riveted on the lone silver light. This was his first glimpse behind the Iron Curtain – even if the little torpedo boat was more than three miles out to sea.

'I was born thirty kilometers away from here – at a place called Parchim. Haven't seen the place since the Russians chased me out as a kid with my parents in forty-five.' Maydag's faded blue eyes flashed back to the instruments; there was no emotion in his voice or face; it was as if the events he described were perfectly normal occurrences.

'Have you never been back?'

Maydag chuckled. 'No fear. Humble first lieutenant as I am, they'd arrest me very quickly – either the Vopos, or the men from State Security.'

'But why?' Mallory asked.

Maydag shrugged a little cynically. 'This job, you know. Our friends over there know all about my occasional trips into the Baltic, and my – er, *passengers*. They know everything, or virtually everything.' Seeing the bewilderment on his companion's face, he went on: 'They know about every naval ship that sails from Kiel, and who's on board. They have spies and petty amateur agents everywhere. After all, we are Germans on both sides of the border; many of us are related, connected by marriage, that sort of thing.'

'You mean, they know about *us?*' Mallory gasped incredulously, as Wismar light began to disappear behind the bucking, heaving torpedo boat.

'Yes, certainly. Their people will have seen you come aboard. They'll be able to describe what clothes you wore and what equipment you carried. Already over there somewhere – East Berlin, perhaps – they'll be analyzing the information, and trying to decide if you're just civilian technicians, engineers, people of that kind checking out the ship – or if, maybe, you're something else.' Maydag chuckled softly. 'Which, of course, you are.'

As Mallory digested this information, Maydag rapped out a swift order, and one of the bridge crew spoke into the voice pipe. The torpedo boat picked up speed and started out into the Baltic, hitting each fresh wave with a shudder that set Mallory's stomach off once again.

'But naturally, if they want to find out who you really are, Herr Mallory, they'll have to catch us, won't they?'

'Do you mean they *chase* you?' Mallory gasped, gawping at the German officer in disbelief. 'I didn't know the Russians did things like that.'

'Oh, yes they do – and more. You see, Herr Mallory, the Russians and their allies, the East Germans and Poles, regard the Baltic as their *mare nostrum*.' He laughed softly, as if at some private joke. 'After all, the whole southern shore is firmly in their hands. Naturally, they don't take kindly to naughty

46

people like ourselves penetrating into *their* sea and landing agents here and there in what was once East Prussia, or further afield in, say, Estonia to find out what's going on. They don't like it at all.'

Mallory was confused. This Baltic business was a whole new ball game for him. 'But skipper, what do you do, if the Russians do turn up?'

Oberleutnant Maydag's faded blue eyes twinkled. 'Run like hell, my dear Mallory. Run like hell...'

The hammocks creaked gently with each roll of the torpedo boat. Hot air, smelling of diesel oil and damp paint, blasted into the tight, fetid cabin from the overhead ventilation pipes. In spite of Germany's booming economy, her sailors evidently roughed it more than their opposite numbers in the Royal Navy. The quarters which now housed the four men of Alpha Team were tight, crowded and primitive. There would be no Miss Linda Lovelace on this trip, it seemed.

But despite the crowded conditions, Sergeant Ross managed to snore. His face looked flushed and angry even in sleep, and harsh, grunted little sounds, not unlike his usual obscenities, came from his open lips. Next to him in his hammock, Rifleman Bahadur, his high-cheeked yellow face glistening as if greased in Vaseline, polished his kukri lovingly, humming softly to himself. Further on, Marine Rogers and Corporal Ramsbottom, the latter stripped to his underwear on account of the heat, conversed in soft, lazy undertones, like men passing away the last hour of the day before sinking into a weary sleep. Otherwise, there was no sound save the soft throb of the turbines and the whirr of the radar screen, as the night fog began to thicken.

Ramsbottom wasn't an imaginative man, but at that moment he felt suspended in time between the happy, if hectic certainties of the last few days, and the unknown to come. Marine Rogers, too, stretched out in the hammock, hands behind his head, gazing at the wire-bracketed overhead light, was obviously a little worried about the future; but being the insecure young man he was, he kept his fears and doubts to himself, leaving it to Corporal Ramsbottom to express them in his own laboured, dogged Yorkshire way.

'You see, Rogers, if the Argies had nabbed us back there in the Falklands, we'd have gone into the bag as POWs. But if the Russians grab us, yer can imagine what'll happen. It could be goodbye for ever.'

Rogers attempted a scornful laugh in the manner of his TV heroes. 'You got your bottle all over the shop, Corp?'

Rifleman Bahadur looked up from his

cleaning, his little slanted black eyes gleaming. 'Bottle', or courage, was an English word dear to his brave Gurkha heart. 'Alpha Team,' he declared proudly, 'Alpha Team – all bottle!'

Ramsbottom grinned easily, showing a mouthful of yellow horse-teeth. 'Right on, Bahadur,' he said, and turned back to Marine Rogers. 'Ner, it ain't that, Rogers,' he explained. 'Yer see, I've got more responsibilities than you. My girl back at Pompey's in the pudden club now. It makes a bloke worry a bit when there's a nipper on the way.' He held up a brawny forearm, rippling with lean, long muscle developed through swimming, to reveal the tattoo there. 'Had that done at Pompey as soon as I heard.'

Rogers stared. It showed the Marine Corps globe, with above, the blue letters of a girl's name, *'Emma'*. 'Hey,' he objected, 'the tattooist ain't got the Marine motto right, *"Always Faithful"*? That ain't right, Corp.'

'He couldn't spell *Semper Fidelis*. Besides, my girl can't speak French, so I thought we'd have it in English.'

Rogers nodded, and his runtish dark face twisted in a sneer. 'What did yer want to go and get her in the pudden club for, Corp? Love 'em and leave 'em, that's my motto. And make sure they're on the Pill.' Rogers frowned heavily, as he tried to find the right words to express his thoughts. 'I mean, a marine in the SBS oughtn't to get himself involved like, ought he, Corp, eh?'

But Corporal Ramsbottom, otherwise known as 'Sheepsarse', remained silent, staring at the metal ceiling. Soldiers going to war must have asked themselves that question since the beginning of time. He certainly had no answer to it.

Now it was dawn. The wind had died to a cold, faint breeze, and a long swell, cold, grey and menacing, rolled from the land. The shore was still visible, but it was out there somewhere, covered by the fog. Now the only sound was the soft throb of the diesels and the wild, rising cries of the gulls as they dived, circled and rose steeply, as if sounding the alarm, warning the world of the intruder in these sombre forbidden waters.

Mallory stood next to Oberleutnant Maydag on the bridge, sipping *teepunsch* – black tea, highly sweetened, with a good shot of cheap rum in it. He shivered and drew the collar of his civilian overcoat closer around his ears. He hadn't realized that the Baltic could be so cold in summer. His feet felt like lead, and the tips of his ears and nose seemed like chunks of ice frozen to his face. He wouldn't be surprised if he got frostbite.

But Maydag was obviously used to it. He was his usual energetic self, sweeping the water all the time with his glasses, barking out orders, correcting speed and course continually, as grey banks of wet, clinging fog swamped them at regular intervals, suddenly bringing down visibility to virtually nil.

'Hot and cold fronts meeting over the coast,' he explained. 'Probably be baking hot ten kilometres inland, but they'll be shivering in their overcoats on the beaches off Rostock. Me, I got a spot in Fort Lauderdale for my holidays. Always get sun there. Going to retire there when I'm sixty. Three thousand marks a month go a long way in the States these days.'

Mallory looked at Maydag curiously over the edge of his mug of steaming *teepunsch*. It seemed strange that a German naval officer should retire to Florida, yet somehow he could understand it. There was something wrong in this place – he could feel it almost tangibly. He could understand how a man who had spent his life in these waters might want to end his days in the sun-baked boredom of Fort Lauderdale and its senior citizens. He shuddered suddenly.

Maydag looked at his pinched, frozen face. 'What's the matter? A louse run over your liver?'

'We say, did someone walk over your grave? But I suppose it comes to the same,' Mallory answered. 'Yes – sort of. This place–' with a sweep of his hand he indicated the grey, rolling clouds of fog and the cold, green, heaving sea– 'It gives me the creeps.'

Maydag nodded. 'A strange place, in which strange things once happened – and still happen. Did you know that days after the old war was over, Soviet and German ships slogged it out in this very spot, fighting it–'

Suddenly he stopped and flung up his big glasses. *'Himmel, Arsch und Wolkenbruch!'*

Involuntarily, Mallory followed his gaze.

Edging its way out of the grey gloom was a sharp-prowed, lean craft, with two 20mm cannon mounted below the radar dome. Mallory didn't need to see the strange craft's flag to know that it spelled trouble – Maydag's face revealed that all too clearly.

'East German,' Maydag hissed, and lowering his glasses, hastily muttered something in German to the man at the wheel. Instantly the engines increased in power and Mallory felt the deck lurch underneath his feet.

'But they can't *do* anything, can they?' Mallory objected.

Maydag gave him a tight little smile. 'Can't they?'

'But we're within international waters!'

'I know. I've taken the utmost care to ensure that we are. But if it came to trouble, it would be my word against theirs. And you know what the lawyers say – one witness is no witness.'

Now the deck started to quiver, and Mallory could feel a thump in the pit of his stomach as the ship rapidly picked up speed.

'We're doing a bunk?' he asked.

'If you mean running away – yes. There'll be two of them. One will try to pin us down, while the other comes in from the sea. We're supposed to feel intimidated because it's two against one. We begin to palaver, and before you know it, they're alongside, signalling that we'd better accompany them back to Rostock – or else!' Maydag licked his lips, which had suddenly turned dry with apprehension. 'It won't be the first time the devils have tried that trick, and it won't be the last.' He forced a tight grin. Behind them, a white bone of foam appeared beneath the prow of the East German boat as it took up the chase. 'And Oberleutnant Maydag can't afford to be booked at this stage of the game. I might never live to collect my pension and stare at all those lovely blue-rinsed matrons in Fort Lauderdale. Here we go!'

Maydag rapped out a quick order, and the torpedo boat's prow seemed to leap out of the water. Suddenly they were hurtling forward at a crazy rate, striking each fresh wave as if it were a solid brick wall. The chase was on!

Mallory gasped. The mist had parted yet

again, and there immediately ahead of them was the other ship Maydag had warned about. The East German craft spotted the torpedo boat immediately. Faintly Mallory could hear the shrill warning of her electric klaxons as the skipper alerted his crew that the quarry had been sighted.

Now a great white wave flew up from her stern. Her starboard guardrails seemed to disappear into the angry, boiling water as she heeled sharply in her turn.

'*Ja, ja,*' Oberleutnant Maydag cried, too carried away by the excitement of the chase to remember that Mallory spoke only a few words of German, '*die Brüder haben uns schon gesehen!*'

Now the West German craft was going all out. Ahead of them was a dense patch of mist rolling southwards. Obviously the other skipper realized what Maydag was going to do. There was a harsh metallic click, amplified a hundredfold, and suddenly a commanding voice called across the distance between the two craft, '*Hier die Volksmarine der Deutchen Demokratischen Republik! Anhalten! Anhalten!*'

Maydag had to shout to make himself heard above the booming voice and the roar of the racing engines. 'He wants us to stop. Not likely!' He tapped his forefinger to his temple in the German fashion to indicate that the other skipper was crazy.

'What'll he do now?' Mallory yelled, as the

54

other craft swung desperately to port, creamy white waves hissing high above her knife-like prow and almost obscuring it.

'Try to cut us off from that bank of fog. And if that doesn't work – well, you'll see, Herr Mallory.'

Now the East German vessel was going flat out, and Mallory could almost hear her prow slapping into the waves, the black smoke from the diesels streaming out in a flat, hard line behind her. She had to be going at at least forty knots – and she was gaining on the slower West German boat! 'Christ,' Mallory cursed to himself, 'get cracking Maydag. *Do it!*' He flung a wild glance at the fog bank. It was still a mile or more away. But Maydag radiated confidence as he stood there on the wildly swaying bridge, yelling orders, shoulders hunched forward as if he were almost physically willing his craft to reach the cover of the fog before it was too late.

Again came a harsh metallic click. Once more the booming voice rang out hollowly over the intervening distance. 'I am ordering you to weigh to *immediately!* You are trespassing in East German territorial waters. Lay to – *now!*'

Maydag ignored the order. Mallory flung a wild glance at the East German boat. Dark figures were running awkwardly along the crazily swaying deck towards the Oerlikons.

'They're going to open fire on us!' he yelled.

'Perhaps they're bluffing!' the German called back, his chest heaving with exertion. 'I mean, there are certain international–'

The rest of his words were cut off by the frenetic chatter of the Oerlikon. Mallory saw the tracer shells come hurtling towards the West German torpedo boat like glowing golf balls, gathering speed by the second. In a blazing arc they spurted over the ship, colouring his upturned face an eerie, unnatural hue. Next instant they had plopped into the sea in front of them, raising huge spouts of crazy, tumbling water that splashed the length of the deck.

Mallory ducked instinctively and felt icy water shower down on his back. The ship reeled wildly. Shrapnel scythed the air. There was the boom of metal striking metal. A radio mast went trailing down, hitting the deck in a shower of spluttering blue sparks.

'Ranging!' Maydag yelled. *'They're ranging!'*

Mallory groaned inwardly. Already he had visions of himself languishing in an East German concentration camp...

But it was not to be. Maydag had sailed these waters too long. The prospect of missing out on retirement in Fort Lauderdale spurred him to fresh heights of cunning.

'Signaller!' he bawled. 'Run up the flags!'

Mallory held on tight as the boat reeled

from side to side and the young German signaller, his over-long blond hair streaming behind him in the breeze, ran up a series of flags. Hurriedly Mallory began to read them, desperately trying to remember what he had learned about them in officers' training school.

First, it seemed that Maydag was challenging the other ship's authority to stop them on the high seas, outside of territorial waters. Now he was agreeing to heave to, provided the other skipper could identify himself and his ship correctly. Mallory flashed a glance to their front. The fog bank was only a few hundred yards away now. Why not risk it? They might just make it – if they were lucky.

Below his feet he could feel the throb of the engines diminishing. Maydag really was slowing down! He was going to let the other skipper come aboard.

'Maydag!' Mallory cried angrily, 'you can't–'

The sudden hiss of smoke-dischargers cut him short. In an instant, rockets were hissing into the air everywhere on the port side of the West German ship, trailing thick white smoke behind them. That very same second the engines surged forward.

Laughing like a crazy man, the tears streaming down his old face, Maydag slapped Mallory on the back heartily, as his ship slid into the cover of the thick white fog, leaving the East German Oerlikons pounding away harmlessly behind them...

4

There were ten kayaks in all, one for each member of Alpha, with another attached containing their rucksacks, weapons and radios. Now, each of them had been lowered overboard, the men clambering after them in the heavy darkness. There was no sound save the lap-lap of the waves against the torpedo boat's hull and the faint breeze in the shell-shattered rigging. All was going according to plan.

On deck Oberleutnant Maydag, whom Mallory had come to know and like during their short voyage together, gave the Englishman his final instructions.

'As far as we know, the stretch of coast you will be landing on is uninhabited. Apparently, not even the Finnish hobby fishermen use it. There are too many mosquitos around in summer.'

Mallory gave a mock moan.

Maydag looked at the luminous dial of his watch. 'Assuming it takes you half an hour to paddle ashore – there is little swell – and another thirty minutes or so to mount the cliffs, you should have about four hours before daylight to get yourself established in a hide without anyone seeing you.'

Mallory nodded.

'I won't start engines for one hour, starting ... *now!* Zero one hundred hours.'

'Zero one hundred, it is!'

'Will you pick us up, Maydag?'

The German shook his head. 'No, someone else will do that, once your mission is accomplished. That's so as to confuse the other side. But,' he lowered his voice, and as they stood there on the gently swaying deck in the glowing summer darkness, Mallory felt he detected a note of affection in it, '*mein Lieber,* you must realize that they know we're up to something – otherwise we would have heaved to after they fired at us. They'll be waiting for us at Kiel when we get back to count our numbers, and–'

'–They'll discover that five crew members – the ones in civilian clothes – are missing.'

'Exactly. So you can be sure that they've told all their vessels in the Baltic to be on the lookout for you. Their land forces, too.' Maydag pointed to the faint, pale glow on the horizon to the east. 'And remember, that's Leningrad over there somewhere – *Russia.*' As he spoke, his face was intent, as if the word itself were a lethal threat. 'I don't know about the Finns. From what I hear, there are very few communists among them; but there will be traitors and spies there, working for Soviet gold, just as there are in my country – and yours, too, for that matter.' For a moment there was a note of bitterness in the German skipper's voice.

Mallory forced a laugh. 'Seems as if it's going to be a right old jolly picnic, doesn't it?'

Maydag laughed with him and held out his hand. 'Good luck, my friend. You'll do it, I know.'

Mallory pressed the hand. It was hard, dry and firm. 'Thank you for everything, Maydag – and I hope you have a good retirement in Fort Lauderdale.'

Maydag gave a hollow laugh. 'I expect they'll call me "Kraut" over there... Sometimes, I think the Israelis should put up a monument to Hitler. At least he gave them a homeland. All he did for his own people was to destroy theirs.' Then he was bending to hold the rope ladder, as Mallory, heavily laden with gear, began clambering to the waiting kayak below...

Mallory breathed in deeply, savouring the spicy scent of wild herbs and pine resin that came wafting over from the land. Now they were paddling into a rocky cove, and the swell was becoming tougher by the second, the waves dashing against the cliff base and surging back in great white combers.

For a moment he rested there in his rocking kayak, while the others formed up around him, all of them breathing hard, save the Gurkha Bahadur, twice victorious in the Devizes-to-Westminster annual canoe race, and Ross, who sneered, 'too much bloody five-against-one, I'll be bound!'

Mallory smiled in the gloom. Trust old Ross; he'd always find something to moan about. 'All right, lads. We'll go in "V" formation, my kayak in front. You back me up, Sergeant Ross and Bahadur. Once we're in, Ross, you'll take charge, while I shin up the cliff and do a recce to see everything's on the Q.T. up there. Clear, everybody?'

There was a mumble of agreement from the rest of the team, except for Ramsbottom, who was their radio expert. 'It'd be better if you could lower us a rope, like, sir, to get them sets up. They're delicate little buggers at the best of times.'

'Will do, Ramsbottom... All right, chaps, here we go.'

With a powerful heave of his shoulder muscles, Mallory shot forward, followed by the others. If he capsized now, he knew he'd be in trouble for the two frail canvas craft were carrying eighty to a hundred pounds of equipment. He'd get more than his feet wet.

Now the little boats were bouncing and skimming wildly across the choppy, heaving water, sometimes plunging deep into the troughs as if they were hurtling down a chute, then rearing upwards once more, supported, it seemed, only by air.

Now Mallory could hear the roar and the slither of the pebbles as the waves hissed and withdrew. Skilfully he fought the kayak round so that he was bellying in a trough directly beneath the cliff, which towered above him in the darkness.

'Here, sir,' Bahadur said, as he came alongside the officer with a few deft sweeps of his paddle.

'Good man,' Mallory gasped and, allowing Bahadur to take care of his kayaks, swiftly undid the canvas top. 'Get ready, I'm going to do my balancing act ... *now!*'

With one convulsive leap, he launched himself forward from the sitting position, hands outspread.

He crashed against wet rock. Madly his fingers sought for a hold on the dripping cliff-face. A sharp outcrop ripped at his nails. One of them came away. He yelped in agony as a burning pain shot through his hand, but held on. 'Got it,' he gasped, not daring to turn round. 'Going up ... going now!'

He reached up and found a tight finger-hole. He heaved, feeling the rucksack tear cruelly at his shoulders; it seemed to weigh a ton. Now he started his painfully slow progress up the cliff-face, while down below, the kayaks danced madly in the swirling water. Foot by foot he crawled ever upwards, searching frantically for finger- and toe-holes in the wet slate, red-hot pincers of burning agony plucking and tearing at his agonized shoulders.

Below, the kayaks disappeared into the darkness. If he fell now, it would be curtains. He didn't stand a chance of surviving a fall like that. Doggedly, teeth gritted, chest heaving with the effort, he crawled on.

At last he made it, and flopped down, exhausted, in the dew-damp, cropped turf, shoulders heaving as if he were sobbing his heart out. He could have lain there all night, but there was no time for that. Already he could hear the first stutter of the German torpedo boat's engines as they started up again. Who knows who might be attracted by the sound of ship's engines so close inland? He had to get cracking. Hurriedly he divested himself of his pack, and taking the rope curled around his left shoulder, began to play it out down the cliff-side. Finally, he attached it to a peg and taking the looped hammer at his wrist, hammered the peg home till he could hear it grate satisfyingly in bed-rock. The ascent could commence.

'All right,' he called through cupped hands, 'up you come. Last man secure the boats!'

Now they all lay sprawled on the cliff-edge, the canvas boats lying all about them, the sound of the torpedo boat's engines ebbing away in the distance as she began her trip back to Kiel, bearing with her the future senior citizen of Fort Lauderdale.

Mallory gave them five minutes while they rested, some of them nibbling chocolate and raisins, some taking a swig of government-issue rum; then he set about getting their camp organized before daylight, firmly barking out his orders. Secretly he knew they weren't really needed; Alpha Team knew the drill backwards – they had done this sort of thing a thousand times or more in long years of training in half the countries of the Western Alliance.

Finally, he said, 'Marine Rogers, you'll come with me. We're going to scout out the immediate area.'

Sergeant Ross mumbled something about 'jammy young bugger', but the rest started on their tasks with a grin. Rogers was notoriously work-shy and a hindrance to the others. He was best out of the way, under the officer's personal supervision.

Together the two of them set off, each armed with his small Polish sub-machine gun. Mallory felt a little silly carrying his. After all, they were in a non-aligned country, and he was unlikely ever to use the thing even if challenged. They came to a stream. Mallory bent and after finding which way the current was running, scooped up a handful of water and tasted it. It was all right. No detergents in this stream. So Maydag had been right. No one was living in the area. It was good to have a supply of fresh water, too.

They pushed on, Mallory noting as they went that the ground was marshy here and there – which perhaps explained why it wasn't farmed. With him leading the way, they headed towards the hard outline of a group of firs which marched across their front like a battalion of spike-helmeted Prussian Guards. Just a quick scout around the edge of the trees, thought Mallory, and that would be that. They'd be safe enough here, at least for the night. Tomorrow, if the coast was clear, they'd find somewhere more permanent to hide up until the word on Fireball came from Cheltenham...

Suddenly a twig snapped to their right. They froze immediately into heart-thudding immobility. Next to Mallory, Rogers raised the machine-pistol. Mallory swallowed hard and whispered, 'No, Rogers, *no!*'

Mallory strained his eyes, his nostrils assailed by a strange raunchy smell like that of someone who hasn't washed for a long time and has done a lot of physical exercise.

Another crack. Again it came from the right. Something or someone was moving in the dwarf birch in front of the pines.

'Christ, sir, what is it?' Rogers whispered nervously. 'It's enough to give a bloke the heeby-jeebies!'

Mallory's right hand, wet with sweat and trembling slightly, reached instinctively for the butt of the WZ 62.

Then suddenly the great shadow detached itself from the trees. A huge four-legged animal was standing there quite calmly, antlered head raised to the breeze. But it was obvious that the wind was blowing straight from the animal to them: it couldn't smell the two men crouched there in the darkness.

Mallory swallowed hard. 'It's an elk, I think.' He cursed his own stupidity. To think that they had been dragged all the way back from the Falklands to carry out a secret mission on the other side of the earth, only to be scared out of their wits by a bloody animal! Angrily he rose to his feet and clapped his hands loudly. 'Bugger off,' he shouted, 'bugger off, you brute!'

The king of the northern forests grunted, and then at a slow lumber, it disappeared into the trees, leaving Mallory feeling like the biggest fool in the Royal Marines.

Now they were bedded down at last. Each man had buried the two kayaks in his charge, removing the turf intact and then replacing it over the hole in which the craft were buried, so that only a skilled observer could have detected that anything had been disturbed. Next, they had set up pangee traps in a circle some five hundred yards in radius all around the camp, camouflaging the holes with ferns and reindeer moss. Any unwary intruder would fall into the hole and impale himself on a sharpened stake, giving out a yell of pain which would alert them. To make sure that animals didn't stumble into the trap, they had rubbed the pointed stakes into the sweat of their armpits; this would act as a warning to wild animals that there were humans about.

Finally they had seen to their own comfort. Each man had dug a hole some three foot deep, in which he had pitched his one-man tent, which was dark green in colour so as to merge easily into the landscape. Then each tent had been heaped with moss so that it took on the shape of the surrounding boulders, and covered with twisted boughs and dry fallen tree trunks, arranged in such a way as to blend with the surrounding swamp. Then and only then were they allowed to bed down for the night.

Now most of them snored, while Ramsbottom, swathed in a camouflaged net which also helped to keep off the mosquitos, his hands and face smeared with the juice of crushed fern in order to stifle his 'human' scent, squatted in the fork of the tree above the hidden camp and did the first watch.

But Roger Mallory couldn't sleep. He was as exhausted as the rest of them by the long day, and he knew he would have to take his spell of the sentry duty in two hours' time yet still he couldn't seem to drop off. The events of the last few days seemed to buzz confusedly around his head. The eternal briefings, the air battle, the near miss at sea – and the uncertain future. Yes, the uncertain future... As he lay there buried beneath the Finnish earth, hardly a sound penetrating from the outside to the hidden tent, he thought of that civilian, with his neat pin-striped suit and bowler, who had first told him his mission during the flight from Ascension to Heathrow. He recalled the man's parting words: 'Remember, Lieutenant Mallory, remember the stakes. If the Huns had caught me back in Poland in those days and I fell into the hands of the Gestapo, my fate would have been simple. They'd have lined me up against the nearest wall. But if you're captured by the Russkis, your end won't be so swift and final. They'll put you in the Gulag.'

'The Gulag?'

'Yes, the Gulag Archipelago. That's the name they give to their concentration camp system. It stretches over half of the damned country, across two continents, Asia and Europe. Once you're in the Gulag, there's

68

no hope for you. It's a living death – and believe me, that's the worst death of all...'

As he lay there underground, as if he were already in his grave, Mallory slowly drifted off into a troubled sleep, with that phrase echoing and re-echoing down the dark corridors of his mind; *'A living death... A living death... A living death...*

BOOK TWO

Fireball!

'Let the boy try along this bayonet-blade
How cold steel is, and keen with the hunger
of blood.'

Arms and the Boy
Wilfred Owen

I

'*Nmetz, tovarisch kommdir,*' announced the armed sentry outside the hospital door, and clicked to attention.

Colonel Bogodan touched his pudgy fist casually to his cap. While the sentry opened the security locks, he took out the bottle of cheap eau-de-cologne that he always carried with him everywhere, shook some on his handkerchief and dabbed it on his brow. Because of his enormous girth, he sweated all the time, winter and summer. But hospitals frightened him and made him sweat even more.

The young sentry opened the door ceremoniously and once more clicked to attention, machine-pistol held rigidly across his chest like an imperial guardsman in an old thirties film. Colonel Bogodan waddled inside.

The room was immediately recognizable as a security ward. There were bars on the windows, filtering the clear Leningrad light, and chains for restraining violent prisoners hung from the walls at regular intervals.

A doctor surrounded by young officers in uniform looked up apprehensively as the huge, fat figure of Colonel Bogodan came shambling towards him, and Bogodan noticed the look of fear with a certain approval. It was just as it should be. After all, he *was* the most important man in Leningrad and the whole Baltic seaboard – more important than the senior mayor and the senior political commissar put together.

The smart young officers snapped to attention, heels clicking on the polished wooden floor, and the doctor held out his hand like the head waiter at the Monopol ushering him to his seat, and said unctuously, 'This way, Comrade Colonel.'

They moved forward down the ward, the doctor in front and slightly to the Colonel's right, the young officers in line behind him, each one carefully observing rank and seniority, as Red Army regulations prescribed.

'There,' the doctor said with a smile, stretching out his hand again like a conjuror producing a rabbit out of a top hat at a children's party.

Hastily Colonel Bogodan dabbed more cologne on his broad, brick-red face, his fat jowls wobbling madly. How he wished he could have delegated this visit to an assistant! He hated this sort of thing – hated sickness and death. He hated the mere presence of doctors. They reminded him just how fleeting life was.

'The German,' announced the doctor.

Bogodan gulped, and his throat was filled with that terrifying, cloying antiseptic odour of hospitals.

The prisoner lay on a metal trolley affair, his body completely naked, his head heavily bandaged. Already the cloth was beginning to turn a pale pink, so evidently the man was still bleeding. An intravenous tube had been inserted in his right forearm, a tube leading to the hanging bottle of plasma in his left. Indeed, tubes seemed to be attached to every part of the dying man, pumping in sodium, glucose and plasma and all the rest of the bone-mender's tricks. With a scarcely concealed shudder Bogodan noted that the poor fellow even had a tube stuck up his penis, presumably to drain off his urine.

Bogodan forced himself to bend down closer to the naked man. The German was pretty old; he could have been in the war. If so, Bogodan would have had good reason to hate him as a former invader. But the German's well-fleshed body had none of the gnarled, twisted scars which indicated old wounds; nor were his feet a permanent ugly red from the frostbite which afflicted the Fritzes in that old war of so long ago.

'Well,' he said, without turning, raising his bulk with a groan of exertion, 'what do you know?'

A young lieutenant wearing the white uniform of the Red Fleet, hair too long and tunic too elegant, and looking to Bogodan's eyes like some damned imperial officer with a private income, his own yacht and a countess for a mistress, stepped up and barked out what he knew at the top of his voice. 'West German torpedo boat, Comrade Colonel... Wreckage indicates one of the *Moewe* class... Apparently struck drifting mine... No survivors save this one... No identification save tunic, Comrade Colonel.'

Bogodan looked at the tattered, burned jacket indicated by the young lieutenant and automatically noted the two tarnished gold bands on what was left of the right sleeve. The dying man was obviously an officer.

Now another young lieutenant took up where the naval officer had left off. He wore the hated field-grey of the Fritzes, but Bogodan judged by his accent and his good-looking Slavic face that he was a Russian attached to the East German Ministry of State Security.

'Comrade Colonel, we in Berlin estimate that the ship in question is the M13. An unfortunate number.' He gave a mirthless chuckle. 'She left Kiel three and a half days ago. We concluded then – a conclusion strengthened by the ship's determined efforts not to stop when intercepted by our own security forces – that she was on some sort of sabotage or terrorist mission in the Eastern Baltic.' He stopped and stepped back smartly.

Now it was the doctor's turn, and by the look of him he could hardly wait to begin airing his knowledge. At first Bogodan could have sworn he was a Jew, but he knew it was impossible; those traitors and people's parasites had been hounded out of the Service long ago. He held up a fat pale hand hastily. 'No mumbo-jumbo, Comrade Doctor,' he warned. 'Just the facts.'

'Yes, of course, of course,' the doctor wheedled, rubbing his skinny hands together and looking more like a Jewish pawnbroker than ever. 'Well, he has compound fracture of the skull for a start. Severe loss of blood. He must have been in the water for several hours, so–'

'Will he or will he not be able to talk?' Bogodan interrupted harshly. 'That's all I'm interested in.'

The little doctor's dark eyes flushed damp, as if he might burst into tears at any moment, and he lowered his head like a bashful young girl. 'No,' he whispered.

Bogodan sucked his lips. 'So we have no further use for him. It is better that it isn't known that he ever existed. Deal with it, Comrade Doctor.'

The little doctor gulped, then clicked his fingers at the burly white-clad orderlies. Hastily Colonel Bogodan turned his back on the naked German stretched out on the cot, while his officers looked at him, obviously expecting a pronouncement. The immensely fat colonel, whose cunning little eyes seemed almost buried in pink fat, was a legend along the Baltic Coast. He had been capturing saboteurs, infiltrators, enemy terrorists – German, Polish, American, British, Latvian, Estonian, Lithuanian, the whole damned pack of them – ever since the days of the Great Siege of Leningrad, long before most of them were born. Bogodan was a fact of life in their world.

Bogodan let them wait. Behind him, the two orderlies started to pull out the tubes one by one. Bogodan quivered. With all those devices clamped to him, the dying German looked like one of those dread creatures he had seen as a boy in those UFA horror films. At last he spoke, ticking off his points on his hairy, sausage-like fingers. 'One, a lone survivor from a German vessel which ran afoul of an old World War Two mine. Two, vessel presumably engaged on an illegal mission. Three,' he stopped short. Behind him on the trolley, the naked German was making low, guttural noises, grinding his teeth as he did so, as if he were determined to fight back death. Bogodan felt the short hairs at the back of his flat, fleshy neck begin to stand erect eerily; it was a most unpleasant sound. With an effort, Bogodan continued:

'Three, if the vessel was landing saboteurs,

agents, the usual sort of paid riff-raff, where have they landed? Fourth, what is their mission?'

Now the dying German was making a strange gurgling noise, thrashing around weakly with his arms, which had now been freed from the restraints of the clamps and tubes.

'*Boshe moi!*' Bogodan groaned, not daring to look round. 'Doctor, can't you finish him off – quickly?'

'I'm doing my best, Comrade Colonel,' the doctor answered hurriedly, and began fumbling for his hypodermic. It didn't do to incur the wrath of the most powerful man in Leningrad. One could easily find oneself mending broken bones in one of those damned Siberian gulags.

'So, comrades,' Bogodan concluded, feeling the sweat stream down his immense inflated body, 'what are we going to do?'

No one answered. They knew it was a rhetorical question.

'I shall tell you. First, there will be a general alert of all naval and land forces on the eastern Baltic seaboard. The militia must be informed, too. Heads of collective farms, village headmen, beach patrols, ferry skippers – the usual stuff. The coastline is long and lonely, and there are too many *new* Russians – people who even after forty years of Soviet rule, still haven't learned where their true loyalty lies.'

Bogodan paused to let the words sink in. They all knew what he meant by 'new Russians': the peoples of the former Baltic States, Lithuanians, Estonians, Latvians, East Prussians, West Prussians, and all the rest of the disloyal scum who still clung tenaciously to their old customs and loyalties – this in spite of the fact that it was over four decades since the glorious Red Army had liberated them from their fascist rulers. Apparently some people didn't know what the word 'gratitude' meant.

Suddenly from the metal trolley came the sound of teeth grating on a tube. Bogodan flinched, his fat face glistening with sweat. What was the Fritz up to now? Why wouldn't he damned well die? But he didn't dare turn to find out.

'The son-of-a-whore is trying to swallow the goddam tube!' snarled one of the order-lies.

'*I fuck my mother!*' cursed the doctor. 'Here, let me do it. *Boshe Moi,* why always me?' There was the sound of something being ripped apart, and then the Fritz gave a soft, long moan.

Bogodan felt his fat legs turn to water. He had to get out of this place before he fainted. 'Comrades,' he gasped hurriedly, feeling the hot bile flooding his throat – why *did* people have to die so noisily? 'Those western swine are up to something. We must stop them. *Dostvedanya.*'

Handkerchief pressed to his thick sensualist lips, little pig-like eyes popping out of his massive brick-red face, he fled for the door.

Behind him, the Fritz's spasms began to subside and the snarling and grating gave way to a succession of soft moans. Finally he was quiet. For good. Oberleutnant Maydag, the man who thought the Israelis should erect a monument to Hitler, would never see Fort Lauderdale again.

'I once knew a bint,' Marine Rogers was explaining to no one in particular, 'who had four nipples – two pairs of tits! Fully developed and all.' He sketched an extravagant curve in the air with his bronzed hands. 'Christ, yer could put yer head between them and not hear a sodding sound!'

Lieutenant Mallory and the rest of Alpha Team were lazing on the beach – all save Sergeant Ross, who was on duty in the camouflaged nest in the tree above their camp, in charge of the radio and surveillance. Mallory grinned at Rogers' reminiscences. Marine Rogers was either a bloody good liar or a swordsman of some repute.

Next to him, Corporal Ramsbottom frowned. Since he had discovered his new 'responsibility', he had no time for Marine

Rogers' obscene small talk. Instead he was constantly trying to 'improve' himself, as he called it. Right now he was busy with the Swedish phrasebook which they had all been issued with in Portsmouth. Swedish was spoken in the border area of Finland, far to the west, and as none of them could be expected to learn Finnish, a notoriously difficult language to pick up, their briefing officer had advised them to learn some Swedish instead. That way, they might fool any Finnish civilians they chanced to bump into. None of them had taken any notice of the advice, save the 'new' Ramsbottom, who spent hours toiling over the phrasebook, laboriously imitating the phonetic script and dutifully learning all kinds of obscure phrases. Now he was savouring the sound of *'Gud in himlen'*, though for the life of him, Mallory couldn't image when the big Yorkshireman would ever need to curse in Swedish. Such things didn't appear to worry Ramsbottom. Only yesterday, Mallory had caught him learning how to say, 'I love you, darling', in that dreary, mournful language; when he had asked Ramsbottom why, the corporal had answered seriously, 'Our lass' – he meant the lady of the 'pudden club' – 'goes for blokes what are cultured, like, sir. I think she'd like me to speak a bit foreign to her, now and again. She says it's romantic *ja sir.*' Mallory had clapped his hand to his forehead in mock-anguish.

Now, his men were enjoying the Finnish summer, in spite of the mosquitos and the wild life in the marshy coastal area, which kept them awake at night. The sea was warm enough for swimming, the air balmy, and so far their Boy Scout existence had been disturbed neither by strangers, nor by anything but routine radio signals from Cheltenham. As Ross had snarled more than once, 'Christ, sir, if we was back in the South Atlantic, we'd be earning gongs by the bucket-load! All we do here is sit on our duffs, getting fat and bluidy stupid, and listening to Sheepsarse blethering away in that ruddy awful lingo all day long.'

All the same, Mallory suspected that even the rough-tough product of the Gorbals wasn't altogether dissatisfied with their life here – especially when he and Rifleman Bahadur were allowed to go fishing of an evening and bring back wonderful, glistening sea-trout and a couple of times, long, juicy eels and mackerel, Ross's special favourite. As the fish were ceremonially placed in the glowing embers of the beach-fire for a late-night snack, Ross's hard, angry eyes lost their customary aggressiveness and positively glowed with delight.

Yet enjoyable as it was to laze their days away in that remote Finnish hide-out, Mallory knew that action would come soon.

Young man as he was, he was not so innocent as to swallow the simplistic picture of Operation Fireball which he had been offered back in the UK by those self-important civvies and his crisp, self-assured, fast-talking senior officers. The Russians would hardly allow one of the most important secret weapons of the future, one which might well alter the whole course of warfare in the next decades, to be snatched from under their very noses just like that. No way!

In those long, lazy off-duty hours on the beach while the others talked and joked around him as if they hadn't a care in the world, Mallory rehearsed various scenarios in his mind. For instinctively he knew that if the slightest thing went wrong, he would be on his own, the sole arbiter of the fate of his little command, deep inside what was effectively Soviet-controlled territory. At best, the Finns would remain neutral; at worst, they would be his active enemies, working with the Russians out of fear and self-interest.

Time and time again, he tried to work out what might happen if things went wrong and they weren't picked up with the vital special parts of the laser satellite in their rucksacks. The most likely result would be a forced march overland, or a trip by sea in the kayaks to the Finnish capital of Helsinki, where he would seek refuge in the British Embassy, leaving the FO chaps the job of getting him, his men, and the parts back to the UK. But supposing the Russians, alerted by their agents in the Finnish capital, arranged for their plane back to London to meet with an unfortunate accident?

There was always Norway, the closest NATO country. But to reach Norway involved a journey deep into Finnish territory, up into the remote north, skirting Russian territory all the time, and across the narrow neck of Swedish land which fringed on the Arctic Circle. Again, how could he be sure that the Russians wouldn't infringe Finnish and Swedish Neutrality, and attempt to stop their flight to safety? Which left the long and dangerous sea journey through international waters down the length of the Baltic, until they reached either Denmark or West Germany; and already he had seen that the members of the Warsaw Pact forces were no great respecters of international waters. As old Maydag had said, the Russians regarded the Baltic as their *mare nostrum* – and they had got the whole damned place sewn up nice and tight.

As the days passed, the men slowly turned the colour of deep oak as they wandered the swampy pine forests or lazed on the brilliant white sand. On the surface they seemed relaxed and at ease, yet already there was a growing mood of tension and unease

amongst them. Now even the most unimaginative of them began to cast second looks over their shoulders as the shadows started to lengthen at nightfall, and often when they were alone in those dark green forests, their hearts would suddenly race at faint rustling noises in the trees. None dared reveal his fears even to his closest comrade, but each one of them knew that soon there would be trouble. Soon there would be trouble...

Less than a hundred miles away, staring down at the happy, carefree crowds strolling in the bright sunshine of the Nevsky Prospekt, Colonel Bogodan sat hunched in his chair, bathed in sweat and lightly stroking his pistol, as he always did when he needed solace in his lonely life. With his pudgy, damp hands he fondled the blue-black metal, perhaps unconsciously trying to rekindle some long-dead erotic memory. What was going on out there, beyond the sparkling green of the Gulf? What were the enemy up to – for they were as much the enemy as the Germans who had once besieged his beloved Leningrad for three long, terrible years.

Once, as a skinny, virile young second-lieutenant of the NKVD, he had eaten porridge made from wallpaper paste, and smeared axle-grease, the only fat available, on the pathetic hunks of bread which had been their staple diet. On that very street down there men, women and children had died by the score and had been left frozen and stacked like cordwood all winter until the thaw had come. Soldiers had fought over the leg of a dog and spent hours trapping rats to eat. His people had died by the thousand.

Now the enemy was at the gate again. He had to defend them. But *how?*

Alone in that big, airy, bright office, Boris Bogodan stroked and stroked, and wondered.

2

The alert, when it came, came with startling, dramatic suddenness.

While Corporal Ramsbottom stood guard and manned the radio link with Cheltenham, Mallory, stripped to the waist and clad in bathing trunks like the rest lolling around him in the burning sand, listened with approval as Sergeant Ross refreshed their memories on emergency medical treatment, SBS style.

'Remember, each of ye is responsible for his oppo. If he cops it, it's up to you to treat him. Not one drop o' drink, if he takes a slug between his knees and nipples.'

Back in training, the 'knees and nipples' bit always raised a smile, but not with Sergeant Ross. The Scot's angry red face and aggressive blue eyes didn't allow for humour – just grim, disciplined purpose.

'...'Cos a bullet going in at the knee might well end up in yer oppo's guts, and he won't want a drink then, will he?'

There was a murmur of agreement from his listeners, who were lounging around him in a circle on the bright white sand. Beyond, the sea shimmered like a green mirror in the hot summer sun. It was a perfect day, light years away from the horrors and sudden death which Ross was describing with such relish.

'Now, what if yer oppo catches a packet in the lower face – say the jaw?' Ross's eyes narrowed. 'What then, eh? He'll have a mouthful o' bits o' bone and gristle and the like. If ye don't watch it, it'll be down his windpipe and choking the poor bugger. So stick in yer fingers and try to whip the muck out. If that doesna work, take yer combat knife and slit his throat right smartish beneath the Adam's apple.' Ross made a slashing movement with an imaginary knife, his eyes gleaming excitedly. 'Then, out with yer ball-point. Break it in two and slip the tube in to by-pass the obstruction. Do it quick and determined and your oppo'll be breathing like a bluidy baby in seconds.'

89

Mallory swallowed hard at the grisly mental picture conjured up by Ross's impromptu lecture; but there was worse to come.

'Yer see, lads,' Ross's nasal Scots voice went on doggedly, 'if you or yer oppo cops it, you've got to keep yer cool. That's the way not to end up looking at the taties from below, ye ken?'

They kenned.

'If yer main artery gets hit, act fast. Don't think. If ye no can catch the two ends, burn yer field dressing and stuff the ashes in the open wound. That'll stop the bleeding. Tie up the wound and forget about tourniquets – bluidy old-fashioned nonsense! Aye, and now for what to do if the wound gets infected. *Puffballs!*'

At the standard lecture back home, Mallory recalled, that had been the occasion for the whole class to stand up and bellow, 'And the same to you, Chiefie!' – which was exactly what the petty officer instructor had expected. It was a way of lightening the grim nature of his lecture.

But not with Sergeant Ross. The men remained sternly silent as he went on.

'...Break 'em open and rub the brown inside on the wound. Acts like yon penicillin. Flies are all right as well. Let 'em lay their eggs on yer. The eggs'll turn to maggots, and the maggots'll eat up all them nasty germs and keep the wound nice and healthy. They say that back in the old days in Borneo, marine Charley Harrison got hit in the guts by the wogs and crawled off into the bush. He lay there four days, letting the flies get at his wound…'

'And that's why they say there's no flies on Marine Harrison!' Mallory interrupted, deciding it was wise to end this nauseating lecture on a humorous note.

Just then, before Ross could react, Corporal Ramsbotton came charging down the beach, still clad in his ankle-length camouflage net to keep off the insects, and looking like a bedraggled green ghost.

'It's come, sir… I'm sure it's come!' he cried, triumphantly waving a message pad in the air and nearly falling over the end of his green net.

'Hold your horses!' Mallory cried, as Ramsbottom skidded to a halt in the sand, flinging back the net from his glistening, excited Yorkshire face and thrusting the message pad into the officer's hands.

Mallory flashed a hurried glance at the long list of numbers grouped in fours and immediately knew instinctively that Ramsbottom was right. Never before had they had such a long message. Usually, the daily signal from the UK had been a routine couple of lines. But this definitely wasn't routine. He snapped his fingers urgently, and Ramsbottom drew out the decoding tables and a pencil. Mallory went to work immediately while the others clustered around him curiously, the holiday mood engendered by the sun and the sea vanished. Now they were the hardened professionals again, waiting like highly-trained thoroughbreds, tensed at the post, champing at their bits, as the starter prepared to give the signal which would send them hurtling down the course. Swiftly Mallory's pencil flew over the groupings, spelling out the message as he decoded.

'...Splashdown definite now... Anticipate parachute descent off coast of Finland... Gulf of Finland between Viborg and Kotka, sixty degrees ... by thirty-two... Approximately twelve miles... ETA ... zero four hundred hours... Thirteen, eight, eighty-two...'

Mallory looked up suddenly. There was a tense silence – no sound save the soft lapping of the waves beyond and the excited breathing of the men. He stared at their tense, sweating faces. 'So this is it, lads,' he said, his voice dry and a little harsh. 'We're in business. It's going to be tomorrow morning.'

'Tomorrow morning!' the words were echoed on all sides. *Tomorrow morning?*

Mallory waited patiently for a few moments, and when he spoke again, his voice was confident, crisp, and decisive.

'So this is the drill, chaps,' he commenced. 'We now know that Fireball will splashdown tomorrow just before first light, twelve miles south-east of our present position. Intelligence placed us exactly in the right spot. Now, as you know, our job is to get there *before* it comes down, locate it at the double, get the bits and pieces the boffins require and get the hell out of there as quickly as we can. The German torpedo boat will rendezvous with us almost immediately, which means that the whole op is going to require split-second timing. Clear?'

'Clear,' they echoed, each one of them preoccupied now with his own thoughts, wrapped up in his personal cocoon of worries and doubts.

'The boffins reckon that this laser satellite is quite compact – not at all like the sort of monsters you've seen on TV being fired at Cape Canaveral. According to Cheltenham, it'll be some fifty by fifty centimeters across, and weigh perhaps fifty kilos – in other words it won't be too difficult for the five of us to handle as it floats on the surface of the sea.' Mentally he crossed his fingers. If the damned thing sank, that would be that; they hadn't a hope in hell of retrieving it from the bottom of the Gulf of Finland with the time at their disposal.

'Now, I'm a layman in these matters, but this is how the thing is normally guided down – what the boffins call the "terminal guidance system". It works either by light from the earth itself, or by radar. One of these two usually controls the retro-rockets used to guide the satellite to a landing. Apparently, the Russians use light from the earth with this laser cannon of theirs. But as soon as our boffins see that the thing is aborting, they're going to switch it on to our radar and bring it down *exactly* where we're waiting.'

'Cunning buggers, aren't they,' Ramsbottom breathed admiringly.

'Wouldna trust 'em as far as I could throw 'em,' snorted Ross.

For his part, Rifleman Bahadur looked understandably blank. All this high technology was a far cry from the simple, black-and-white world that he knew. Only Marine Rogers, the untaught electronics genius, remained unimpressed. He listened to Mallory's simple briefing with a look of growing doubt on his ugly, pimply young face.

'...So in essence, we're going to steal the flying cannon from under their noses. As soon as we've located it and picked it up, we'll remove certain vital parts, of which I have a list, plus take as many photos of the whole thing as time allows.' He smiled at them. 'Quite simple, really. A quick smash and grab, almost.'

Marine Rogers looked distinctly doubtful. As the others chattered excitedly among themselves, he raised his hand like a schoolboy asking to be excused. 'Sir,' he said, trying to attract a smiling Mallory's attention. 'Sir ... please.'

'Yes, what is it, Rogers?' Mallory asked easily.

'Well, sir, I don't really know how to begin...'

'At the beginning?' Mallory suggested.

'And slap a bluidy "sir" on that, Marine Rogers!' Ross snorted, eyes glowing angrily.

'Well, sir,' Rogers began awkwardly, 'I don't think it's gonna work out quite like you said.'

'How do you mean, Rogers?'

Now the centre of Alpha Team's attention, the Don Juan of Pompey was strangely embarrassed. He actually blushed beneath his tan. 'Well, sir, although the Russians might use light, as you say, they'll also monitor the satellite with radio or radar at the same time – or so I should imagine. So as soon as the thing aborts, they'll start to react. And I bet their tracking equipment is as good as ours,' he ended almost defiantly.

There was a pause while the others absorbed what he had just said. Sergeant Ross flashed him a murderous glance, but the young pimply Marine ignored it.

'It stands to reason, don't it, sir? They could be on the scene as quick as us.'

Mallory said nothing for a moment. The same doubts had plagued him back in the UK. *Wouldn't the Russians react immediately,*

once they learned the laser satellite had aborted?
The boffins' answers had been fulsome, winning, but not altogether convincing: ... of course, the Russian tracking system will go into action once things start to go wrong up there – of course, my dear Lieutenant Mallory. But naturally we'll have the edge on them. By the time they start to react, you and your fine young men will have collared the bits and pieces and be speeding back to Kiel in the torpedo boat. No doubt about that, old chap. Mallory felt a stab of unease. The boffins had blinded him with bullshit, but he mustn't let the men know that.

'I doubt it, Rogers. We're right on the spot. They'd have to scramble air and water to find the satellite. By the time they had a fix and got going, we'd be finished with our task and on the jolly old torpedo boat.'

But still Rogers wasn't satisfied. He stuck doggedly to his guns. 'But, sir, what if they have something like us, sir? A kind of Russian SBS.'

'Aye,' Corporal Ramsbottom chimed in now. 'If they did, they could put in a heliborne frogman force, just like we would. They might not be able to reach the spot on time but they could drop them in our path while we're on our way to rendezvous with the torpedo boat. If they did–'

'If ma Aunt Fanny had a moustache,' Sergeant Ross sneered angrily, 'she'd be ma

Uncle Jim! What a bluidy bunch of nervous Nellies! I've never heard so much blether! Like a lot o' ould wives!' He straightened to the position of attention and turned to Mallory, his face brick-red with anger and contempt, leaving Rogers to mumble and pout and Ramsbottom to look worried. 'What's the drill now, sir?' he barked.

For once Mallory was grateful for Sergeant Ross's bullying, no-nonsense attitude. 'Three things, Sergeant.' He beamed at his listeners. 'One, a good swig of Nelson's blood to celebrate.'

There were smiles at that. The Gurkha licked his cruel, thin lips in anticipation. He dearly loved his rum, though no one yet had ever really seen him drunk. 'Rum give bottle,' he announced in his fractured English. 'Plenty rum, plenty bottle.' He rubbed his skinny stomach to show exactly what he meant.

'Two,' Mallory continued, 'a damn good feed. We'll eat up everything we've got left, except for our iron rations. And three, a darned good kip til zero one hundred hours. I think tonight we can dispense with sentries.'

A couple of minutes later they stood in a circle in the hot sand, their faces – even that of Rogers – wreathed in smiles, as Mallory raised his canteen of rum and water.

'Lads, I'd like to make a toast. To the success of the Fireball mission, and a speedy return to Pompey!'

The men of Alpha Team raised their canteens: *'To the success of the Fireball mission, and a speedy return to Pompey!'* they bellowed back.

Startled by the noise, the seagulls stomping stiff-legged on the sands rose in sudden flight, crying in hoarse protest at these bold, bronzed young men standing there upright and confident, so confident of success...

3

The night was ideal for their purpose. A gentle breeze caressed the darkened waters. Soft ripples fondled the shingle. Here and there, the dull orange rays of a summer moon shone through the heavy banks of cloud, illuminating the spiked outline of the fir-fringed Finnish coast and enabling Alpha Team to get their bearings.

Linked together by their toggle ropes, the five kayaks, with one empty canvas canoe in tow to take the loot from Fireball, moved south-east at a steady, even pace, heading out into the Gulf. In the lead, Bahadur, who had the keenest eyesight and hearing of them all, paddled effortlessly, swinging his head from right to left, routinely scanning the horizon for the least sign of danger. But there was none. It was as if they were alone in the world, just the five of them, puny mortals set in this vast, limitless, lonely sea. It was the bleakest stretch of water that Mallory could recall. Even the South Atlantic Task Force, which had taken such great care to ensure that its route to the Falkland Islands remained secret, had encountered at least two ships. Here, in the Gulf of Finland, it seemed there wasn't a single vessel afloat.

Somehow it was both disquieting and re-assuring. At least there would be no chance of their being spotted and a swift radio mess-age being sent to the Communist-held shore. And in this breathless stillness, where the only sound was their own laboured breathing and the soft rustle of the wind, they would be able to hear the throb of the West German torpedo boat's engines from miles away.

Now it was well past midnight, and they were already quite close to the place where the all-important Soviet laser satellite would splash-down. So far, everything was going exactly to plan. A cynical little voice in the back of Mallory's mind told him it was perhaps going a little *too* smoothly, but he hushed it with a silent curse and turned his thoughts back to the task in hand.

After the effects of the rum had worn off, he had begun to consider the operation more carefully. He had started by dividing his little force into two sections. Corporal Ramsbottom and Marine Rogers, his two technical experts, would be responsible for dismantling the satellite and removing the bits and pieces the boffins back in London so desperately wanted. He, Sergeant Ross and the Gurkha Bahadur, would spread out from the site of the splash-down and take over perimeter security, armed not only with hand weapons, but also with a little surprise item given to them by the MOD at the very last moment: a mini-secret weapon recently developed by the Ministry's scientists, consisting of a small plastic mine that exploded with devastating effect when it came into contact with an enemy vessel, and also gave off a thick cloud of white smoke. It was the ideal device for a clandestine sea-borne op of this kind. All the same, Mallory hoped they would never have to use it. It would be far better for all parties concerned if the pick-up went off without trouble.

Ramsbottom's fear that the Russians might have their own equivalent of the SBS continued to worry him. Supposing they did; although they might not be able to reach the site of the splash-down in time, they could easily stop the West German torpedo boat escaping with its precious cargo – even if it were in international waters. Of course, the mission was a vital one, and the risks had to be run; the SBS couldn't let themselves be frightened off by a few Russkis. All the same, speed was going to be essential: a quick snatch, and then off.

Suddenly Mallory chuckled to himself. Once he had been stationed at the US Naval Base at Peniscola – a name that gave rise to much amusement among the men. In the town there had been a big break-in at a local store, and the base newspaper had run a shot of the wrecked window under the headline, BIGGEST SNATCH IN TOWN HISTORY. That had really set the cat among the pigeons. The editor responsible had been dispatched to Vietnam forthwith.

The thought of those happy, carefree days training with the US Navy somehow re-assured Mallory. He returned to the present and the task ahead of him with renewed confidence and energy. It was a beautiful night. Nothing was going to go wrong. Nothing *could* go wrong...

'*Nyet, nyet, tovaritsch!*' the naked whore screeched at the Militia captain. 'On the head of the Black Virgin of Kazzan, I swear it ... *I didn't kill him!*' Desperately she made a grab at his arms, but he dodged and indicated to the militiaman standing guard on the whore's bedroom door to restrain her. Then he looked over to Colonel Bogodan, who was leaning against the wall, panting softly like an old dog exhausted by the summer heat, and shrugged. Bogodan nodded his approval wearily, gently stroking the hard, powerful, comforting length of the pistol in his trouser pocket.

This was a case for the Militia, a routine death; but when foreigners were involved, as now, Bogodan always liked to be present. Idly, he stared around at the whore's room, at the mirror attached to the ceiling above the rumpled bed; at the cuddly teddy bear which all whores seemed to possess; and lastly, at the very dead fat man, with a limp prophylactic hanging from his member. It was, Bogodan noted, coloured black.

Typical decadent Westerner! Unconsciously, Bogodan stroked the hidden gun a little faster. They all came here to Leningrad to see the port built by Peter the Great; a quick gallop round the Ermitage, and then it was off to the Prospekt to pick up one of those tall, cool, blonde Baltic whores – so vastly superior to the dowdy, dyed trollops of Moscow. And all of them brought their decadence with them – their jeans, their hideous music, their Coca-Cola. Well, this one had paid for his degeneracy.

'I didn't mean to give him an orgasm like that,' wailed the whore. 'How was I to know it would croak him, Comrade Captain?' She wrung her hands in a gesture that reminded Bogodan of the movie stars in the old days. 'Russian men *like* it that way… Foreigners

102

are not so strong, I should have known.'

'Shut up!' snapped the Militia captain, now busily sifting through the dead man's clothes.

Bogodan noted with disgust that the foreigner wore a little silver chain around his neck like a damned silly woman. In sudden irritation, he took his pudgy hand off the pistol, grabbed the whore's imitation silk gown and tossed it to her. 'Here, woman, put this on!' he commanded. 'Showing your tits like that!'

'What a way to go, eh?' the Militia captain grinned, as he came across to Bogodan bearing the dead man's wallet. 'Still, there's something to be said for it, Comrade Colonel. Killed in action, you might say.' He grinned again.

Automatically, Bogodan returned the tough young policeman's grin, but he felt little real amusement. Before the captain had been born, hundreds of men had been killed in *real* action in this very same street. In that grim December of '41, you didn't die in bed with whores, that was for sure.

'American,' the Militia captain said, holding up a green passport.

Bogodan nodded without much interest.

The policeman leafed through it for a moment, then tossed it back on the bed.

In the mirror above, Bogodan could se the whore stuffing her breasts into her gown while the young policeman guarding her stared with undisguised interest. Unconsciously, Bogodan's pudgy hand fell once more to his pistol and he stroked it urgently.

'Comrade Colonel.'

The Militia captain was holding up a small piece of stiff white plastic, decorated with the encircled eagle of the US Department of Defense, with the man's photo in the right-hand corner and the letters 'NASA' stamped across it in a bold red.

Bogodan immediately forgot the whore and his pistol. He snatched the card out of the policeman's hand. 'He worked for the American government?'

'Yes, comrade Colonel. For their space agency.'

'Is he with the American Embassy, then?' Bogodan rapped.

'No, comrade. As you know, the American diplomatic pass is a different colour from the normal one, a bluish colour.' He stopped and waited, conscious of the fact that it didn't do to be too pushy with the gross, sweating man with the pudding face opposite him. In Leningrad, Colonel Bogodan made the decisions – even the most lowly militiaman knew that. A snap of Bogodan's fingers, and the unfortunate victim of his displeasure could say goodbye to the good life of Leningrad; Siberia would beckon.

While the Militia Captain indicated to the

man at the door to get rid of the pale-faced whore, Bogodan thought aloud: '...Not a diplomat, but working for an American government agency... Following the usual tourist route – port, picture-gallery, pornography...' With a wave of his pudgy hand he indicated the overhead mirror, then frowned thoughtfully, pursing his bright-red, sensualist lips. 'Genuine, or false? Look at it from the Americans' point of view. Would they risk someone who might have secret knowledge up here, so far away from their embassy in Moscow? As everyone in that decadent country knows, Russia is a dangerous place, full of spies and beautiful secret agents out to seduce the unwary and the innocent.' He allowed himself a pale-eyed grin. Immediately the Militia captain smiled too – it was safer that way. There was an old peasant saying: 'When the Tsar says crap, you crap!'

'...Why risk him, therefore?' Bogodan mused. 'What is there to interest a space agency man up here?'

This time the question wasn't rhetorical, and the Militia officer, though badly out of his depth in these matters, felt obliged to make an attempt to answer it. 'Red Fleet HQ out at Oranienbaum, Colonel?'

Bogodan shook his head, and his jowls wobbled, noisily. 'No, their missile ships wouldn't interest a man like that.'

'Our own anti-missile air defences for Leningrad?'

'*Nyet!*' Bogodan snapped, a little angry now. '*Gavorit,* this man wouldn't be interested in conventional missile technology! At NASA they work on the big ones – the ones that go into outer space!'

The Militia captain stared at his highly polished jackboots. His knowledge was exhausted. 'I'm sorry, I can't help you, Comrade Colonel.'

Bogodan flashed him a little smile. 'I didn't expect you would, my dear fellow. Never fear.' He tapped his temple with a fat forefinger. 'The old wooden head will come up with something. All right, clear up the mess here, comrade Captain. Send me a full report as soon as you get back to your office in the morning – and don't plant the American yet. Put him on ice. We might need him still.'

'And the whore?' He jerked his thumb to the door, where the woman waited in the dark, smelly corridor. 'Deportation order, comrade Colonel?'

Bogodan looked at the naked man on the bed, whose sightless eyes still stared up at the mirror. For a moment he allowed himself to picture the scene: the fat American below, his overworked heart bursting as the orgasm wracked his body; the whore on top, riding him in a wild gallop to the death...

Instinctively, Bogodan's crept towards the hard length of his pistol. For a moment he forgot the missing five civilians, the dead Fritz from the boat, the degenerate American, and considered his own problem. A whore like that who could ride a man to death, might...

Hastily he abandoned that particular train of thought. 'No,' he commanded, 'put her inside the cooler for a few days. I might – er – need her for questioning...'

'*Da!*' the Militia captain snapped, springing to attention, hand touching his high peaked cap.

Hastily Bogodan acknowledged the salute, and as he did so, the Captain noted to his surprise that the fat man with the moon-like face was blushing.

Quietly, riding the lane of moonlight, they bobbed up and down on the water. Together they formed a circle some fifty to a hundred yards in diameter, and each member of the team had been allotted a different section of the compass to search.

It was a beautiful night, the stars twinkling a bright silver in the velvet backcloth of the sky. Never before had Mallory realized just how many of them there were in the heavens. It seemed as if the whole world were asleep except the five of them riding out the slow, lazy troughs in their kayaks, and those tiny yellow objects in the night sky so many hundreds of miles away. The silence and the peace of it all lent a strange, unreal atmosphere to the whole operation. Could it be real? Mallory asked himself for the umpteenth time. Could they really be sitting here, behind the Iron Curtain, waiting for a weapon of the future to come plunging out of the sky so that they could gather it up and whisk it away to what was another world, as far removed from this one as Venus is from the Earth? It all seemed absolutely impossible.

Twenty yards away, Sergeant Ross gave a light dip of his paddle in the gleaming water, glistening drops trailing from it like a string of pearls as he lifted it again. Easily the kayak glided forward a few paces. Like the rest of them, he was keeping perfect station, automatically going into 'lowest position', sliding forward and down into the boat, so that from a distance he might be mistaken for a floating log.

Mallory nodded his approval. In spite of the unreal quality of the scene, his men were sticking to their training techniques rigidly and without orders. If an enemy were sighted, he knew that each man would freeze motionless, stowing the paddles close alongside to allow the tide and wind to carry him clear, as if the kayak were nothing more than a harmless chunk of driftwood. At sea, there were no irregular combat soldiers to match the SBS – and naturally Alpha Team were the cream of the cream.

'Sir!' It was Rogers.

Mallory craned his head round, the canoe swaying slightly at the sudden movement.

Rogers was sitting erect, pointing at the sky to the west of them. High up, a tiny pinprick of yellow light had suddenly begun to fall out of the sky at an alarming rate, a blaze of bright light sweeping after it like a sickle of blood.

Mallory's heart missed a beat. This was it! There was no mistaking it. The boffins had been right after all. Right up until the very last minute he had remained doubtful that they could predict so accurately what was going to happen; that five men could be sent halfway round the world to pick up an object which fell from the sky a hundred miles up. But the boffins had proved him wrong.

'Stand by all hands!' he cried in sudden, almost overwhelming excitement, heart thumping madly as if it might burst out of his rib-cage at any moment. *'Stand by to retrieve Fireball!'*

'What?' Bogodan yelled into the telephone, swinging his stockinged feet off the desk instantly and dropping his beloved pistol in his astonishment. 'What did you say?'

At the other end, the excited KGB liaison

officer at the Oranienbaum Red Fleet HQ repeated his message. '...The Fleet and the Air Force are at alarm state one, Comrade Colonel. Everyone is ready to go wherever needed. But I don't think – with all due respect – that it has anything to do with us.'

Bogodan's brain raced as he slumped there over the phone. A trickle of sweat dripped from his brow onto the metal top of the desk. It was stiflingly hot in Leningrad – perhaps that was why he couldn't sleep. But no – that wasn't it. It had been the sight of the whore and the dead American with the rubber hanging from his limp member. 'Hard as frozen cod,' she had breathed before they had taken her away. 'It was too much for him...'

With an effort Bogodan forgot the whore and tried to piece together the bits of the jigsaw puzzle – the missing civilians, the dead Fritz, the American from Nasa...

The solution suddenly hit him with terrifying clarity.

'*Boshe moi,*'he exploded over the phone to his subordinate. 'Listen to me, and listen carefully if you want to live to be a year older! I can't give you reasons, so don't ask. But that satellite that's out of control – there's more to it than meets the eye. Tell the admiral that Colonel Bogodan says he must alert the Fleet for sea duty at once. Further, he must ensure that the eastern

Gulf of Finland be sealed off *immediately!*... Listen, I don't care a wet fart about the admiral's sleep. Wake him and give him those orders. If he objects, tell him Colonel Boris Bogodan says it'll cost him head and collar if he fails to do what I say. Now jump to it, man!' And he slammed down the phone before his subordinate could object further.

Hurriedly he began to tug on his boots, sweating profusely. Outside in the harbour, he could see the first pink tinge of dawn above the flat stretch of dark green. Soon it would be light. There was no time to waste.

4

Now Rogers and Ramsbottom worked feverishly at the ditched satellite, as it floated on the surface, tangled among the drag chutes. From his position some fifty yards off, Mallory could just see their dim outlines, illuminated by the torches as they removed the heat shield and anti-radiation baffle and burrowed into the innards of the experimental weapon.

Now his lethargy and feeling of unreality of earlier on had vanished. He could feel every nerve tingling with excitement. His heart beat was racing; adrenalin rushed through his bloodstream. He had never felt so alert, so wide awake, so fully alive. It was as if he had drunk a whole bottle of bubbly in one quick go. It was a heady, perhaps even potentially dangerous feeling. He told himself he had to keep cool.

Mallory flashed yet another look to the east – to Russia. Already the horizon was beginning to flush pink, breaking up the velvet darkness of the night. Soon it would be dawn, and another hot day. It wouldn't be long now before the West German torpedo boat appeared, ready to carry them back to Kiel.

There was a harsh click. Mallory turned, startled, thinking that two men stripping the satellite might have run into some technical difficulty. But the sound didn't come from Ramsbottom and young Rogers; it was Sergeant Ross, paddling softly some twenty yards away. Mallory could see him clearly outlined against the pink light of the dawn. He had cocked his WZ 62 and laid it carefully on the canvas deck of the kayak in front of him.

'Trouble?' Mallory called softly.

'No, sir,' Ross answered in the same quiet way, as if he, too, were anxious not to disturb the tranquility all around them. 'Just a precaution, sir. Ye never know in this world.'

Mallory smiled. Trust Ross. The tough

noncom would probably welcome a bit of a barney.

The minutes ticked by. Mallory began to feel the strain. His eyes ached as he searched the horizon to the west for the first stark outline of a speeding torpedo boat and the rapid white blink of a signal lamp. The knot was in his stomach again. Even though it was only four in the morning, he promised himself that the moment he was aboard the Jerry torpedo boat, he would wrap himself around the biggest and stiffest drink their wardroom could provide!

'Lieutenant, sir!' came an urgent whisper. 'Ship ... it comes.' It was Bahadur. He was sitting upright in his canoe, pointing west. 'I hear.'

Mallory couldn't hear a thing. He tried the old trick of cocking his ear to the direction of the breeze. Yes, there it was! The throb of a ship's engines. The Gurkha had heard it long before the rest of them. It had to be the torpedo boat.

'Good for you, Bahadur,' he called, and then to the two men bent over the floating satellite, 'Hurry it up over there on Fireball. Our ship's on the way!'

'Five minutes, sir ... just five more minutes,' Ramsbottom called, his voice strained, as if he was gritting his teeth.

'All right, but on the double!' Mallory turned to Bahadur and Ross. 'You two –

113

close up!' he ordered, no longer whispering. There was no need. They were almost home and dry now. 'That way, we'll form a bigger area for identification.'

'Shall I set off the smoke flare, sir?' Ross asked.

'Not just yet,' Mallory said after a moment's thought. 'Better not give away our position until we've identified them.'

'Right, sir.'

It was only long afterwards that Lieutenant Roger Mallory realized just how fortunate that snap decision had been.

Now the sound of racing engines was getting louder by the instant. To the east the pink tinge was beginning to turn a vivid blood-red, with the sun about to appear over the horizon at any moment. Then they spotted it: a long, lean shape, low in the water, completely blacked out, not a single navigation light showing, as if this were the Baltic of 1942. Mallory felt his mouth go dry. It was their contact all right. He recognized her lines. She was of the *Moewe* class, the same type as the craft commanded by Oberleutnant Maydag.

Now the West German ship went into a great, fast curve, and Mallory saw a sudden burst of white against the black water as she turned. She had begun her search. Soon her Aldis light would commence signalling and he would order Sergeant Ross to fire the signal flare. But he would wait one more minute. The torpedo boat was still a mile off. He didn't want to give his position away too early.

'Stand by to fire flare, Ross!' he called, as the boat came ever nearer.

'Finished, sir!' Ramsbottom called.

'Start stowing the bits and pieces!' Mallory ordered.

Now all was tense anticipation. Behind Mallory, Rogers and Ramsbottom fumbled feverishly with the strings of the canvas bag in which they would carrying the vital parts of the laser cannon, while the other three, paddling backwards, swung in towards them, eyes fixed on the approaching ship, faces painted a harsh red by the first rays of the ascending sun.

And then, suddenly, as when a brain snaps into madness, it happened. Abruptly all was noise, violence, hate – death. The lone helicopter took them completely by surprise. One moment the sky was empty; the next, the chopper came hurtling in low over the sea, almost as if it were sliding across the waves, violent light rippling from both sides, its missiles already hissing towards the torpedo boat like a flight of fiery red hornets.

Violently, the skipper swung his craft round, sending up a great flare of wild white water. The ship heeled madly, its wireless mast almost touching the water. The first flight of missiles flew harmlessly over the ship's deck.

The black helicopter bearing the blood-red stars of the USSR clattered above the heads of the Alpha Team, deafening them with its roar, the rotors throwing up a great sucking wind. Alpha Team fought the water madly with their paddles, as huge suction waves reared up on all sides. For a moment, both helicopter and ship were lost to sight in the tossing, heaving sea. Then they were there again. A petrified Mallory, his face bathed with sweat and spray, stared in amazement as the dark figures of the German ratings pelted across the deck towards their Oerlikon, while the helicopter swooped in for another attack like an evil black raven.

'Heck, sir!' Ramsbottom cried in his plaintive Yorkshire accent, 'They can't do that! It's international waters!'

'Silly cunt!' Ross yelled, one hand clutching his paddle, the other the little Polish sub-machine-gun, 'Of course, they fucking well can… *Look!*'

Just as the first German reached the twin cannon turret, the helicopter dropped out of the sky like a stone, the heavy machine-guns located on both sides of its black fuselage chattering frenetically. Bright-green and red tracer streamed down towards the torpedo boat below, as the German skipper flung his craft into another desperate curve. Slugs howled the length of her deck. Even at that distance Mallory could see the ugly little bursts of blue sparks as they struck the armour plating and tore into the helpless German gunners. The first man staggered, hands clawing the air as if climbing the rungs of an invisible ladder, before slamming down to the deck. Another whirled round and dropped – and another. Then once more the helicopter went zooming up into the blood-red sky, leaving the deck below littered with heaving, twitching bodies.

Mallory groaned. It was standard attack procedure. Knock out the gun crew first and then work the defenceless ship over. Now only damned good luck and some decidedly tricky manoeuvres would save the German ship.

The skipper obviously knew it. Again he flung the craft around in a tight curve, a wild white wave streaming out behind him. Then he immediately veered into another curve to port, to put the helicopter off its aim.

But it was not to be. The Russian out-guessed the German. As the torpedo boat broke to port, the 'copter was already there, waiting for it. Like a lethal hawk, it hovered there, rotors ruffling the sea below, whipping it up into new frenzies.

Mallory tensed. This was it!

'Brave bastards – for Jerries,' Ross

admitted grudgingly. 'They could have done a bunk, but they didna.'

There was a sudden rush of sound like an express train hurtling through an empty station at a hundred miles an hour. Furious lights flared under the chopper's body. One ... two... The missiles went hurtling towards their defenceless target.

Mallory found himself digging his nails into his palm till it hurt. Drenched with sweat, he waited for the inevitable...

The missile exploded in a searing flash of incandescent white light at the side of the German ship. For one long, agonizing moment, the spectators in their canoes were blinded by the terrible glare. Then they saw the scene in all its horror.

The German torpedo boat was sinking fast, her hull rearing out of the water like a terrible, nightmarish white whale. Burning oil was streaming from her ruptured tanks in an ever-growing circle of red, through which panic-stricken black shapes, some already half-consumed by that monstrous blowtorch of flame, could be seen attempting to swim, their strokes growing weaker by the second. Overhead, the helicopter hovered, its fuselage bathed in the eerie red light from below, its gunners tensed and waiting for anyone to break from that circle of fire. But no one did. One by one the screaming, shrieking sailors went under. There was no need to waste bullets on them.

Still the hull raged out of the flames. A lone figure could be seen scrambling up it wearily, like a climber nearing the summit. Mallory willed him to get there and survive, but it was no good: beneath him, the dying ship gave a long, low groan like a despairing, resigned animal that knew its end was near. She shuddered wildly. Then, with startling suddenness, she was gone, sliding beneath the waves and leaving behind her a flurry of excited white water and bubbles exploding obscenely on the surface. Where once there had been a ship, now there was only the crackle of the flames and the deafening clatter of that sinister bringer-of-death hovering overhead.

How long Mallory and the rest of Alpha Team squatted there, not moving, not thinking, Mallory never knew – perhaps it was only seconds. At that instant it seemed an age. Then suddenly, as the chopper started to turn, the sun glinting from its cockpit, Mallory woke up to the danger they were in.

'Go! Go!' he cried, above the sudden racket as the chopper picked up speed. 'It's spotted us!'

'Bugger that for a tale!' Ross cried.

While the others started to streak at a tremendous rate across the still, glistening water, leaning low over their canoes, paddles slicing through the waves, Ross swung round and faced the enemy racing down on them, a latterday David ready to meet a mechanical flying Goliath.

Within seconds the helicopter was on to them. The world was filled with the hectic clatter of rotors. Suddenly the sea was lashed into crazy fury. Tracer zipped through the air. All around Ross, the water erupted, and he could feel the heat as the tracer whizzed past him. Undeterred, he took aim, balancing as best he could with the kayak bobbing up and down on the waves.

'Get a feel o' *that!*' he snarled, his red, angry face set in a wolfish grimace. He pressed the trigger. At this side, the little Polish sub-machine gun burst into frenetic life. Bullets hissed up at the helicopter rearing over him. Suddenly little pieces of black metal were raining down on all sides. Violently the chopper swung round, smoke streaming from its fuselage. Now the pilot brought it in at almost wave-top height. Ross could see the white blur of the pilot's face beneath his visored helmet as he came in for the kill.

Ross waited calmly, his canoe rocking wildly on the crazy sea. He knew exactly what the Russian would do: he would roar in close then break to left or right, so that one of the gunners – who were already hanging out of the doors on both sides of the chopper, machine-guns at the ready – could blast the lone figure below out of the water.

'Not on yer nelly, you Russki bugger!' muttered Ross, and raised his sub-machine gun. Already he could feel the prop-wash whipping his clothes tight about him, dragging the very breath from his lungs and making him gasp for air like an asthmatic in his death throes.

The chopper loomed ever larger, filling the sky. Now Ross could see every detail of the pilot behind the sparkling Perspex, as he hunched over his controls, gloved hand clutching the stick. Ross's knuckles turned white on his trigger. He couldn't miss now. He gasped and pressed the trigger. The little automatic pounded in his hand. Gleaming yellow cartridge cases flipped hissing into the sea. His nostrils were assailed by the stink of burnt explosive.

Suddenly the Perspex of the helicopter's cockpit shattered into a gleaming spider's web of cracked plastic. Blinded, the pilot raced overhead, while Ross sent a hail of slugs into the under-belly of the black monster. There was an angry hiss of red-hot escaping oil as it hit the wild waves. At that height the temporarily blinded pilot hadn't a chance of bringing the crippled chopper up.

Gasping for breath, hardly noticing the oil burn that ran down the left side of his face, Ross watched mesmerized as the chopper hit the first wave. For a moment it seemed that it would make it, bounce free. But then suddenly it tilted to one side. A rotor hit the water and broke off immediately. Completely off balance, the chopper swung round crazily. Ross caught a glimpse of a panic-stricken Russian, mouth open wide in a silent scream, and then it was gone beneath the waves. A sudden fury of white, boiling water, and it had vanished completely, the circle of black oil extending ever outwards, as if it would never stop until it reached the ends of the earth...

Now Mallory in the lead could hear the thunder of surf breaking, and knew that his calculations had been correct. They were approaching the estuary of the river west of the coastal town of Kotka, which ran into the great central Finnish lake system just south of the remote township of Heinola. Already he estimated the tide was carrying them along at about four knots.

He flung a swift glance at the coast to starboard. Along what was probably the promenade at Kotka, he could see lights burning. Soon, as the sun flooded the coastal town, they would be extinguished, but for the time being the place still slept – which was all to the good. He wanted to be ashore and making plans on what to do next before they were spotted by the Finnish authorities.

The men of Alpha Team bunched together in their frail craft in order to hear Mallory's orders. Ahead of them the water was beaten to an angry white froth, and Mallory, slightly in the lead, could see they were approaching a tide-race: a fierce tumbling of water, tearing over rock or sandbanks. It was going to be an ordeal, especially after the long night's work and that terrifying airborne attack.

'Now, listen to me!' he yelled above the wind and the roar, 'close up, and remember: all you have to do is to carry out your normal rough-water drill! You, Bahadur, close up to the rear – just in case!'

Bahadur, the best canoeist among them, gave the thumbs-up and grinned.

Mallory attempted to look equally cheerful, but failed lamentably; he had too many problems on his mind.

Hastily the men of Alpha Team secured their cockpit covers, before turning their canoes head-on into the tide-race. Almost immediately, the canoes trembled and shook like live things as they drove into the wild, boiling surge. Now the SBS found themselves fighting water like they had never fought it before. Paddles flailed. Shoulder muscles heaved left and right. Time and time again they were blinded as the flying spray struck them in the face like a cold, wet fist. At one point Ross went under, but came up again, spluttering and red-faced.

'I help, Sarge!' Bahadur cried, shooting forward to the struggling, cursing noncom.

'Get yer bleeding brown paws off me, Gungha Din!' Ross bellowed, highly indignant that anyone should have the temerity to offer him, Sergeant Duncan Ross, assistance. 'What d'ye think them stripes are? Fucking Scotch mist!'

Bahadur grinned, in no way offended, and expertly steered his canoe between Ross and the tidal race to give him a moment's breather.

On they raced, fighting their way through the white horses, bows lifting and dropping, paddles flailing as they struggled to keep head-on, every muscle and nerve straining to keep their body balance, their shoulders ablaze with agony at the effort. The tide was running so fast that it felt as if they were thrusting their paddles into thickening cement. Each new sweep took a super-human effort. Sweat streamed down their faces. Their mouths hung open like those of stranded fish, gasping for breath. Once Mallory thought with a thrill of fear that he was done for. A great wave caught him and flung him to one side as if he were a matchstick. He caught his startled cry of fear just in time. Next moment, Bahadur had appeared from nowhere, battling against the angry, hissing waves and throwing his canoe bodily against Mallory's, nudging him back into the head-on position. The ordeal went on.

Now they were racing into the narrows where the estuary met the sea. Mallory had fleeting glimpses of white-painted cottages to port, with fishing nets hung up outside to dry; but whether they were inhabited or not, he had no time to see. He was too busy trying to fight his way that last hundred yards or so that separated them from the calm water beyond.

A sudden cry rang out above the roar of the water. It was Rogers. A hard splash – and in he went, his canoe capsized. But already Bahadur, his dark face glistening with sweat, was going all out to the struggling young marine. With all his strength he slammed into the empty canoe. The blow sufficed. It drove the craft towards Rogers, who didn't need a second chance. Reaching out frantically, he grabbed the canoe and hung on desperately like a frightened infant clinging to its mother, allowing himself to be driven forward by the racing tide, while Bahadur acted as escort.

At last they were all safely through. Collapsed over their paddles, they gasped for air, shoulders heaving as if they were sobbing their hearts out, while young Rogers noisily coughed up sea-water. For some minutes while they recovered, they simply allowed themselves to drift gently up the river, the roar of the tide-race disappearing behind them, drifting, drifting into the unknown...

Now they were cut off behind the Iron Curtain. There was little prospect of help from the neutral Finns, whose lives were under constant threat from the red giant just across the water and before them lay a trek of nearly four hundred miles to the nearest NATO territory. Even as he slumped there, wracked with pain, fighting to control his hectic breathing, Lieutenant Mallory knew he must think – and think fast – if he was ever going to bring Alpha Team home alive.

And so they drifted on, five puny mortals adrift on a lonely remote river that bore them ever northwards to the lakes, and to the wild, brutal, snowbound country that lay beyond...

BOOK THREE

Hell-Country

'Prepare you, generals.
The enemy comes on in gallant show;
Their bloody sign of battle is hung out,
And something to be done immediately.'

Julius Caesar
Shakespeare

I

'Well, Bogodan, and what is your guess?' enquired the Moscow general, giving the fat, sweating Colonel Bogodan a smile which revealed excellent teeth.

Hastily Bogodan felt in his pocket for his pistol, and reassurance. The Moscow general was everything he wasn't: young, handsome, elegant, his hair turning grey at the temples and giving him that distinguished look that so appealed to the women. To Bogodan's envious eyes, he looked all too virile.

Bogodan tried to collect his thoughts. 'The facts first, comrade General. Those western bandits have obviously stolen key parts of the laser satellite. The plan obviously was to rendezvous with the Fritz torpedo-boat, which as you know, had that unfortunate accident with – er – a floating mine from World War Two. There seem to be a lot of them about.'

'Serves the Fritzes right,' remarked the General. 'They sowed most of the damned things in the first place.'

'Agreed, comrade General. Now, before the pilot of the Red Fleet helicopter met his death, he reported that he was attacking five civilians in canoes. I have good reason to believe that these were the men who stole the parts of the satellite and were to rendezvous with the Fritz ship.'

'*Horoscho!*' said the Moscow general, politely enough, 'this I know. Now, your surmises?' And he touched his Hero of the Soviet Union medal, won for his recent intelligence activities in the South Atlantic.

Bogodan noted the gesture. The general had been helping those damned Argentine greasers, who had now thrown in their hand and let the British walk right over them. Obviously he was very proud of it. Bogodan sniffed. Why, *he* had a whole drawerful of tin back home that would make the general's eyes bulge from his pretty face with envy! Or would it? No – in his heart of hearts, he knew that the Moscow general would envy nothing that he – poor, fat, impotent, sweating Bogodan – possessed. The Moscow general was one of the winners, the new men, their heads full of all this new-fangled, technological stuff. He was yesterday's man, a relic of an old, forgotten war, who held onto his position by the skin of his teeth, because he still had power here in Leningrad, and because he didn't fail – too often.

'Surmises? Well, comrade General, here are some of them. First, these damned civilians might make an attempt to contact their embassy in Helsinki.'

'But there are many such western embassies in the Finnish capital, Comrade Bogodan. We can't watch them all.'

'We don't have to, comrade,' Bogodan replied. He pulled open his drawer and took out a small khaki-coloured tin. 'Pudding,' he announced, using the English word, 'coming from the English Army's compo combat rations, found near the site of the splash-down. Conclusion?'

'That the only embassy that needs watching is that of Her Majesty, Queen Elizabeth,' the Moscow general announced triumphantly.

Bogodan frowned. 'Yes,' he said, and squeezed the pistol even harder. The swine was just too cocky for words. 'Perhaps, however, these English bandits will not take that risk. What then?'

'The sea route. If they are skilled canoeists, which they seem to be, I don't suppose it would be too difficult to clear the Finnish and Swedish coasts hopping from island to island, until they reached, say, Norway.'

Bogodan waited with apparent patience until he could destroy the Moscow general's argument. 'Exactly, comrade General,' he said ponderously, when the other man had finished. 'There is, however, a defect in that proposition.'

The Moscow general frowned. 'What?'

'These English terrorists witnessed the

131

unfortunate accident suffered by the Fritz ship in international waters. Would they risk a similar accident to themselves – even if they hugged territorial waters?'

'I see what you mean. *Davoi*, comrade Bogodan. What do you guess, then?'

'This.' Bogodan poked a fat finger at the map spread out on the desk in front of him. 'Finland,' he barked, encircling that country with a wave of his finger. 'Here, as you see, about six rivers almost cross the country from south-east to north-west, where Finland links with Sweden, and here, further north, with Norway. Now all those cross-country rivers pass through the central Finnish lake system – here.'

'I understand.'

'Now, if these people *are* skilled canoeists, and if they want to avoid contact with the Finns – which is probable, since they are in that country illegally – what do you think they might do, comrade General?'

'Use the river system?'

'Exactly.'

'But which river?'

'It doesn't really matter,' Bogodan said easily.

'What do you mean?'

'Well, all these rivers flow through the Finnish lake system, as I've said – in particular, through Lake Pajanne, where it narrows to a kind of straits just below the small township of Jyvaskyla – here.' Bogodan stabbed the map with his forefinger, indicating an area covered with a rash of blue marks representing water. 'That is the bottleneck through which anyone using the river system must go before he comes to the lakes beyond, and finally to the coast and Finland's borders with Sweden and Norway.'

The Moscow general nodded his understanding. 'I take your point, comrade Bogodan. This place, er, Jyvaskyla – what damned impossible names those blubber-eaters have over there – would be the ideal place to stop them, *if* they were to use the river system, as you seem to think they might.'

'Yes,' Bogodan said laconically, and waited.

'But how can we do that – I mean, if you *were* right? After all, although we exert a great deal of influence on Finland, we can hardly expect the blubber-eaters to apprehend our own criminals for us, can we?'

Again Bogodan contented himself with a laconic grunt that might have meant anything.

'And how could we put our own people in? Sooner or later, the Finns would get onto them as they marched north, and then there'd be one hell of a stink. We've only just dodged one in the Falklands. If it ever leaked out just how much we helped the greasers – well…' The general stopped, obviously wondering if it was wise to confide even this

133

much to his colleague. For a moment he fingered his enamel medal nervously, as if reassuring himself that it was still there.

'We could go in by air. Drop some special troops on those straits, well away from the township, and like the spider, just wait for them to walk into our little trap,' said Bogodan. He still wasn't quite ready to spring his final surprise; he knew the other man would try and pick holes in his suggestion, and was waiting excitedly for the inevitable objection. He would dearly love to take this handsome, virile young Muscovite down a peg or two.

'Paras. Naturally, but you are forgetting, my dear comrade,' the Moscow general said patiently, 'radar – *Finnish* radar! They'd pick our plane up even before it had passed our own coastline. Up would go their Saabs, and that,' he shrugged eloquently, 'would be that. No, I'm afraid that won't do, Bogodan.'

'But there are planes and planes, Comrade General,' Bogodan said cagily, preparing to let the other man have it between the eyes.

'What is that supposed to mean, comrade Colonel?' the Moscow general said sharply. Bogodan could see by the look on his pretty mug what he was thinking – that old Boris Bogodan was no longer up to his name; that he was in his dotage: a willing horse who should be put out to pasture. 'There is no plane on this earth, capable of carrying paras which could escape detection by enemy radar.'

'But there is,' Bogodan persisted, springing his surprise at last. 'Have you never heard of a glider, comrade General?'

The Moscow general's mouth fell open stupidly. At that moment Boris Bogodan could have hugged him in triumph and delight.

Their hide was close to a small, marshy creek, some five miles up the estuary. Just as they had sailed into it and had begun covering the kayaks with reeds and moss, they had almost been surprised by a small fleet of ancient chugging motor-boats laden with nets and crewed by sleepy, scruffy men in blue, most of them smoking little clay pipes and chatting softly to one another, as men do in the early morning when they are not quite awake. Evidently they were local fishermen going out for a day's work at sea.

That had been four hours ago, and since then they hadn't seen a soul – only a great white kingfisher which had been stalking majestically through the reeds before it spotted the men hiding there and rose with a great clatter of wings and a squawking noise. Now, recovered from the ordeal of the night, they squatted under their camouflage nets covered by the six-foot-high baking hot reeds, eating cold stew and hard biscuits, and washing the meal down with sips of tepid water from their water bottles – for Mallory had already imposed a water and food rationing system.

Mallory was feeling the heat. Beads of sweat glistened on his furrowed brow as he studied his map of Finland and the Baltic, every so often flinging a glance at the patch of brilliant blue sky above his head, as if he half-expected another Soviet chopper to come racing down, machine-guns chattering.

'Look, chaps,' he said finally, 'I'll be frank with you.' They turned and stared at him, their faces an ugly red from the heat under their camouflage nets. 'Our only hope of getting back to the UK is a hard slog cross-country – most by kayak, as I see it, though we might have to hoof it some.' He stared around at them. 'And we'd better not fool ourselves. We can't trust anyone we might meet en route – Finns or Swedes. Perhaps when we get to Norway, it'll be different. But for the time being, every man's hand is against us.'

'You're right there, sir,' Ross said heartily. 'Bluidy wogs – I wouldna trust 'em as far as I can chuck 'em!'

'I wog,' Bahadur said happily, recognizing a word frequently used by the men of Alpha Team.

'Ah yes,' Rogers said, 'but you're not yer

typical wog, see, Bin. You're an honorary gyreene. One of us, like.'

Bahadur beamed even more.

Mallory shook his head in mock-wonder at the perverse logic of his men, and continued. 'And we all know what'll happen to us if we're nicked by the Russians. We saw that this morning when that chopper attacked the torpedo boat, and then us.'

'Curtains,' Ramsbottom said laconically.

'Curtains,' Mallory agreed. 'We mustn't kid ourselves on that score. We know too much. We'd have to be silenced for good. I'm glad you all understand that, because it means you know we can't give up, whatever happens and however tough the going gets.' He paused to let his words sink in, and stared solemnly at their red sweating faces. He was reassured and gladdened by what he saw there; his men were tough. They wouldn't let him down.

'Now, I have little – no, let's be honest – I have *no* knowledge of what lies before us, except that we'll be travelling through the same latitude as Northern Norway, just below the Arctic Circle. And we all know from our Arctic training in Norway what to expect even at this time of the year.'

'Aye,' snorted Ross, 'bluidy freezing weather. Freeze the goolies off a bloke!'

'Exactly, one has to watch one's outside plumbing exceedingly carefully up there.

Not only that, our rations are running low. There's only our iron rations left.'

'How long do you think it'll take us, sir?' Ramsbottom asked.

'As long as the weather stays like this, we'll make good time; later, not so good,' Mallory answered. 'I'd give us a week. But I don't think we'll starve. We've all had survival training – we know how to live off the land.'

Rogers, who liked his food, moaned. 'Christ, not them bloody boiled worms again!'

Everybody laughed, and Bahadur rubbed his stomach. 'Worms good ... make Gurkha randy!'

Mallory held up a hand for silence. 'All right, you know the worst. At dusk we strike north.' He smiled. 'Into the unknown, as you might say.'

But his attempt to lighten the mood was lost on them; if anything, they seemed to become even more solemn.

Ramsbottom confided. 'Er, if you'll excuse me saying so, sir, I think I speak for all the lads when I say we've got a lot of confidence in you, sir.' He looked at Mallory in a very direct manner, a serious look on his broad, honest Yorkshire face. 'If anyone's gonna get us through, sir, it'll be you!'

Mallory lowered his gaze hastily, suddenly oddly moved. 'All right ... er, carry on, chaps,' he said. And unusually for him, there

138

was a slight tremor in his voice.

On the first day, they made good progress, though for most of the time they were forced by the current to paddle close to the banks of the river, uncomfortably conscious of the noise of their dripping paddles, longing for wind or rain to deaden the sound. For they were far too close to roads and small white-painted villages for comfort; occasionally they could even see people wandering about, engaged in the daily tasks of rural life.

Once they were startled out of their wits by the sudden noise of a motorboat starting up, and barely managed to dart into a clump of high reeds before it belted past them at high speed.

'Just remember,' Mallory had tried to reassure them, 'those Finns might well take us for holiday canoeists, or something like that.'

But Ross hadn't bought it. 'Holiday canoeists?' he had growled. 'Five grown men, one of them black as the ace o' spades, paddling regulation Mark II canoes? My eye!' And he had spat grumpily into the brown water.

Their second day started off badly. Within minutes of setting out, they were confronted by a six-foot cliff of soft, slimy mud to negotiate, and then another stretch of the same before they could get their canoes launched once more. Ross and Mallory fought their way up the cliff first, and hauled. Then the lot of them followed, wading thigh-deep through oozing, slippery mud that stank to high heaven and had Bahadur twittering nervously, apparently afraid of creatures lurking beneath the surface of the mud. Thereafter they fought the kayaks to the water, pushing them across the soft ooze, arriving at the river plastered with mud and wet through. Mallory heaved a sigh of relief when at last they were able to push off again. He had been convinced that the sounds of their boots squelching through the mud must have alerted everyone for miles about.

Now the heat of the coast started to give way to cooler weather, with a brisk, fresh wind blowing in from the north-east. The sky, too, had changed from a leaden sultry grey to a hard, cold blue. Mallory was conscious of the fact that soon they would run into the cold of the north, even at this time of the year. But there was one consolation; as they pushed ever nearer to the Finnish lake system, the villages thinned out. That afternoon, for example, they only saw people on the shore twice, and the few inhabited places they passed were safely away from the river, as if the water were frozen over most of the time in winter and therefore of no use to the villagers.

That night they slept fitfully. Almost as

soon as they had set up their hide in a clump of tall reeds, plastered with mud, a thin, cold rain started to fall, which made it difficult to cook and sleep, even though they had paddled some ninety miles in the last two days and were bone-weary.

The next morning they awoke to find that frost had formed on their wet clothing, and as they rose stiffly from their nets to meet the new day, their clothes cracked and squeaked as if they had been starched.

Rogers yawned, scratched his unshaven chin, and brushed away a trace of white hoarfrost from his bushy eyebrow, before shivering dramatically. 'Bloody hell, it ain't half cold!' he announced to no one in particular.

'Yer get yer bluidy share o' it,' Ross snarled, urinating in a cloud of steam into the water of the creek. Bahadur, meanwhile, performed his obscure morning religious ritual.

Mallory rubbed his eyes free of sleep, reached down as if for water to clean his face and then thought better of it. Better stay dirty and warm than clean and cold – that was what they had always said in survival school. Evidently it was a doctrine with which the traditionalist Sergeant Ross didn't agree, for already he was embarking on his 'ablutions', as he called them, stripped to the waist, washing and shaving himself in the icy water of the creek. Mallory shivered again and left him to it.

That afternoon, the wind was still icy cold in spite of the thin, watery sun. The river began to broaden slowly but surely, and Mallory guessed that they were now heading into the first of the lakes which were a feature of this part of the country. He ordered the men to close up, and in a tight file, each man unconsciously adopting the timing of the man in front of him, they paddled steadily forward to the great stretch of shimmering blue-green water, fringed on both sides now by long stretches of Douglas pine and quick-growing firs. The only people they would come across up here would be lumberjacks employed in the forests, which was something to the good.

It was about six that afternoon, just when Mallory was beginning to think that they had had enough for one day and should start looking around for a hide for the night, when Bahadur, keen-eyed as ever, spotted the boat. He had been following the flight of a great 'V' of wild duck, waiting to find out where they might land; for wild duck were easy to catch and cook. But unfortunately they disappeared to the west, their place taken on the horizon by the unmistakable outlines of a ship.

Immediately, they paddled furiously for the nearest cover, all exhaustion forgotten, hearts thumping wildly, the adrenalin pumping into their bloodstreams and giving them a burst of fresh energy. For a good half hour they crouched among the reeds, surveying the craft, which lay slumped like a stricken animal near the bank half a mile away, while the sky overhead slowly changed to an ominous, snow-laden grey.

Even at that distance, the hidden watchers could see that some of the craft's plates were missing, giving her the appearance of a stranded whale with its bones showing. Nor was there any sign of life on board. Not a whiff of smoke came from her crooked funnel, or from the rear where the galley would be. Through his glasses Mallory scanned the scuppers where dirty water would emerge and the lake around for signs of floating trash, paper, cans and the like. But again there was nothing. He made his decision.

'Chaps,' he said, 'I think she's abandoned … and it's going to be a bloody cold night again. I think we should sleep there tonight. I know it's not the drill taught at the survival school, but the survival school wallahs are probably sleeping in nice warm beds tonight. We're not. So I say, let's forget the drill.'

This time, even Ross had no objections.

With the watery yellow sun beginning to disappear below the stark, spiked horizon and the sky growing even more leaden and threatening, they paddled cautiously forward to the ship. Tonight they might be hungry, but at least they would be warm.

Slowly, the first, sad flakes of snow began to drift down.

2

As always in Mother Russia, Colonel Bogodan found himself hindered by bureaucracy and red tape. Three days passed before he could get his clandestine operation approved by Moscow. Even the Moscow general, who was one of the seven deputy directors of the KGB and was widely tipped for election to the Central Committee the next time one of its present septuagenarian incumbents died, couldn't hurry things along. Russia was still ruled by obscure clerks – men who could never change their routine or step out of line. No wonder, Colonel Bogodan cursed to himself more than once during those three days, 'hurry slowly' was a Russian saying. It had been true ever since Rurik had first set up a Russian state.

But at last the ancients of the Central Committee had roused themselves sufficiently from their permanent doze to give their approval. The op could go ahead.

Thus it was that Bogodan found himself

facing the tall, lean commander of the Red Eagles in the control tower of Schlusselberg Military Field. Hurriedly Bogodan gave him his last-minute instructions, while outside the towing plane warmed up its engines, ready for the night flight, and ground crews attached the wartime glider to the nylon towing rope.

Major Gusiev, dark, saturnine and obviously Georgian to judge by his jet-black hair and flashing, dark eyes, was clearly less than delighted with his mission. He and his Red Eagles were veterans of clandestine operations in Afghanistan and Angola, as he had explained testily to Bogodan on the car journey to Schlusselberg. They were para-commandos – and they were not accustomed to flying in 'contraptions made from canvas, held together with glue, and taken from the Red Army's War Museum!'

The major had been wiser than he knew. Bogodan had searched high and low for a suitable craft, until the one used by war-time glider-borne troops had been found in the War Museum. What a commotion it had caused among the bureaucrats when Bogodan had demanded it for 'special purposes'! The director, purple-faced and heavy with war decorations, had nearly had a heart attack, and had threatened to write to the Central Committee in protest.

But now all was ready. At this moment

Bogodan was too elated to be worried by Major Gusiev's doubts.

'Listen,' he lectured him, while behind them, the computers clicked out the latest weather forecasts for Central Finland, details of wind speeds at various altitudes and other information for the two pilots, 'during the war, eighteen-year-old boys, who'd learned their gliding in two-week courses with the Young Pioneers, landed freight gliders at this very spot – under artillery fire! There were hundreds of them, landing mostly at night, too.'

Major Gusiev was not impressed. 'May I remind the comrade Colonel,' he said, icily correct, 'that this is not the war. That glider is a decrepit wreck, and it will be carrying not stores of war, but men. Finally,' he snapped, 'none of my Red Eagles knows the first thing about glider-landing.'

'Well, give them a quick course during the flight,' Bogodan answered angrily. Why was it these days everyone seemed to think he was as obsolete as that damned glider out there? Hurriedly he grabbed for his pistol, needing its comfort. 'Now, you know the drill. Once you have made the landing at the chosen spot, you must deal with the bandits as quickly as possible. The longer you wait, the more likely you are to be discovered. We must at all costs avoid an international incident with the blubber-eaters over the water.'

146

'Blubber-eaters?' Gusiev echoed, puzzled. 'Oh, you mean the Finns. Yes, yes, I understand. But you must realize, comrade Colonel, my Red Eagles can't work miracles.'

'I know, I know,' Bogodan said impatiently. It seemed that even these young specialist killers were as bureaucratic as any damned Moscow pen-pusher. 'But you're landing in a virtually uninhabited area – just the odd wood-cutter and a few hobby hunters, that's all. You shouldn't have any trouble finding five Englishmen there, especially in the strait.' He passed on quickly, not wanting to hear any more objections. 'As soon as you have carried out your task, you will contact our people at the Helsinki Embassy. They will arrange for you to be picked up by private car, returned to the capital and flown out by Aeroflot the same day. In other words, Major Gusiev, my estimate of the duration of the whole operation is forty-eight hours from the moment you land in Finland.'

'If you say so, comrade Colonel,' the tall airborne major said, but his voice lacked conviction.

'I do,' Bogodan snapped, pressing the hard metal of the pistol with a sweaty paw. He forced a smile. 'And remember, comrade Major, there will be promotion and a suitable decoration in it for you, plus special rations and special leave for your Red Eagles...'

That seemed to do the trick. The major straightened up proudly, shoulders back, and there was a misty look in his eyes, as if he could already see the Secretary of the Central Committee pinning the Hero of the Soviet Union medal on his chest. But almost instantly his proud posture was deflated by the worried voice of the tug-pilot behind him. 'By the great whore, it's snowing over Central Finland!'

Major Gusiev spun round. 'What did you say, Lieutenant?' The worry in his voice was all too evident.

The tug-pilot snapped to attention and repeated the message, holding up a computer print-out as evidence.

Gusiev flashed Bogodan a look. 'Did you hear that, comrade Colonel?'

Bogodan was tempted to snort, 'Do you think I'm dead as well?' but instead smiled winningly. 'I'm confident that you have the best men available in the Air Force. They won't let you or your Eagles down, I'm sure.'

'It won't be easy,' the glider-pilot said hesitantly. He was only a sergeant in the Red Air Force, but he had been a champion glider-pilot in the Young Pioneers before being called up for military service. 'Gliders are difficult to handle in snow... Thermals are particularly bad...'

Bogodan glared at him, eyes menacing,

148

daring him to continue. The pilot, intimidated, fell silent. Bogodan turned to Gusiev. 'Well then, Major, are you ready?'

'Yes, comrade Colonel.'

'Good, then let us go.'

The pilots collected their papers, and Gusiev picked up his assault rifle. Together they stepped out into the darkness. Beneath each perimeter light, an armed sentry stood guard. Bogodan had ordered the place to be completely sealed off for the start of the clandestine operation. Security was so tight that even the base commander didn't know the true purpose of the glider's mission.

The antiquated craft had now been attached to the jet and its sides packed with thermite grenades which the Eagles would ignite once they had landed. This would mean that the Red Army's museum would lose its precious exhibit, but Bogodan had seen to it that the bemedalled director would never know. Already the KGB's secret workshops were busy building an exact replica.

Outside, after the heat of the day, it was cold. Even Bogodan felt it through his layers of fat, and shivered. Already, it seemed, another damned winter was on its way. He quickened his pace, and in the glare of the reflected light, watched as Major Gusiev lined up his Eagles, all dressed for the purpose of their mission in shabby civilian clothes and wearing blue-peaked caps of the kind worn by Finnish workers. Even the nondescript clothes couldn't completely conceal the fact that the twenty-odd men now preparing to enter the ancient glider were the élite of the Soviet special forces. Every one of them looked like a trained athlete, and Bogodan could see from their proud bearing that they were top soldiers, too. They had an animal-like alertness that came from much hard training and action. As Gusiev gave a low order and his Eagles began to file into the plane, Bogodan felt confident that no one could win against such fellows – least of all five decadent Westerners, as the bandits undoubtedly were. The British hadn't a chance.

Now the jets of the towing plane began to whine ever louder. Behind it, the glider started to tremble quite violently, and the young sergeant-pilot at the controls seemed to have difficulty holding it; it was as if the ancient war-horse had sniffed the scent of gunpowder again, and was eager to charge to the sound of the guns for the last time.

Bogodan smiled. It was a good sign. Now he knew everything would work out well. Soon, in that little inner circle of Intelligence, they would once more tell of 'old Boris's' brilliance, and of the remarkable feat he had masterminded in the wilds of Central Finland.

Major Gusiev strode over to where Bogodan was standing, the wind from the jet whipping his clothes about his fat frame. Gusiev saluted very formally.

'Comrade Colonel, permission to move out?' he barked, his breath fogging on the cold night air.

'Permission granted, comrade Major,' Bogodan answered, trying to muster what was left of his military dignity. 'Good luck to you and your brave Eagles, my dear fellow. We must celebrate when you return to Leningrad.'

The tall, lean major grunted something, then swung round and marched straight-backed and proud across the tarmac, as if he were stomping across Red Square on the Day of the Revolution, to announce the parade to the Central Committee.

Five minutes later he and his men were gone, and all that could be seen of them were two red lights winking in the velvet darkness.

Bogodan, watching there all alone, was suddenly overcome by emotion. He dabbed his handkerchief to his eyes. What brave boys they were! Sadly he turned, handkerchief in hand, and waddled back to the waiting *Zis*.

They had wandered all over the beached ship by now, staring in wonder at the shell-pocked superstructure, and creeping through the jammed, leprous steel of the bulkheads, covered with diseased fingers of yellow fungus.

Mallory stared at the grotesquely twisted rails, the charred woodwork, the bullet-holed poop and the rest of the mangled steel remains.

'Must be a relic of the Russo–Finnish War,' he declared.

'Did they have a crack at the Russians, sir? The Finns, I mean?' asked Rogers.

'Twice, in fact. Once in 1939, when the Russians invaded them. Then again in 1941, when they invaded Russia with the Germans. That's why the Finns have a healthy respect for the Big Bear.'

As the snow had started to fall more thickly, they had hurried below into the interior of the long-abandoned vessel, happy to be under cover at last, especially on such a grim night. Now they squatted in what had once been the radio shack just below the bridge, amid a shambles of shell-shattered dials and valves and torn wires hanging from the ripped-open grey enamelled cabinet. Some smoked fitfully, preparing themselves for the serious business of sleeping. Ross, as always, was already asleep and snoring lustily.

For his part, Mallory read, tucked inside the comforting warmth of his sleeping bag. It reminded him of his childhood – that feeling of being cosy and snug in bed, protected from the elements. Outside, the wind was howling in the shattered rigging, a door was banging in the breeze, and the snow was pelting down furiously. Tomorrow Mallory knew he would have to face up to the problems the snow brought with it, but for the time being he preferred to forget them. With the hood of the sleeping bag up around his ears, he read by the flickering light of a stump of candle, which he had found in his search of the ship.

He could hardly have brought with him a more suitable book for this night, and this place; Erskine Childers' *The Riddle of the Sands*, with its account of high adventure and espionage off the North German coast in the days of the Kaiser. He re-read the section at the beginning of the spy adventure, when Carruthers, the hero – how typically named! he thought – tells Davies and Bartels how he had failed to enter the Royal Navy:

...And I can't settle down to anything else. I read no end about it, and yet I am a useless outsider. All I've been able to do is to potter about in small boats. But it's all been wasted *till this chance came. I'm afraid you'll not understand how I feel about it; but at last, for once in a way, I see a chance of being useful.*

Mallory raised his eyes from the page of his

battered T. Nelson and Sons edition of 1903, and stared round at the yellow faces of his men, revealed by the flickering light of the candle. How apt those words were for him! There was no other life for him, but the Marines – more precisely, the SBS. He could have had an easy life in the City, with plenty of birds, fast cars and fancy lunches in smart restaurants and all the rest of it. He had plenty of money, had been to the right schools, had the right contacts. He was ideally equipped to become a man about town. But it wasn't him. This was his life – chancing his neck in the arsehole of the world, backed up by a handful of men who were as devoted, tough and as loyal as himself. He was sure that if his pals back home could see him now – unwashed, unshaven, the only food in his stomach a bar of chocolate and a handful of raisins – they would have laughed out loud and told him what a bloody fool he was. But at this particular moment he wouldn't have changed places with them for all the fancy menus at Mirabelle's and the smartest, sexiest popsy in town.

Suddenly he forgot *The Riddle of the Sands* and his reflections. From outside there came a strange sound, louder than the wind, a kind of sharp hiss that he couldn't quite identify. He dropped the book and looked up. The others did the same.

'Did you hear?' Mallory asked sharply.

'Yes, sir,' Ramsbottom said, alert written all over his broad face. 'It sort of comes and goes, like.'

There was a moment's silence, broken only by Sergeant Ross's snores, as they all strained to listen to and identify the queer hissing noise.

Mallory made a decision. He hated to leave the comforting warmth of his down-filled sleeping bag for the icy cold up top, but there was nothing for it. 'Wake up Sergeant Ross. Rifleman,' he snapped to Bahadur, 'come with me.'

Swiftly clambering into his boots and pulling on his thick navy-blue pea jacket, Mallory clattered up the twisted, shell-pocked stairs and into the whirling white night. 'Bahadur, you take starboard, I'll take port. Sing out if you hear anything.'

'Yes, sir,' Bahadur answered, as if he were back on the barracks square, and clattered away to carry out his task.

Cautiously Mallory ventured out of the cover of the overhanging superstructure and into the flying snow. A little helplessly, he narrowed his eyes against the snowflakes. It seemed like a complete white-out. He could hardly see more than a couple of yards, except when the wind changed direction at odd moments and the whirling clouds of smoke seemed to part; then, he could just make out the snowbound shore, and beyond, the dark silhouettes of the firs, already packed heavy with snow. Who the devil could be out on a night like this, he asked himself, feeling the snowflakes lash his face like a thousand icy razorblades. It was impossible. He strained his ears, but could hear nothing.

'Sir!' It was Bahadur's voice coming from the other side of the ship.

'Can you hear … see anything?'

'Think so, sir.'

Mallory doubled around the deck, springing over the rusting steel scrap and once nearly slipping on the slushy snow that was beginning to pile up everywhere. He found Bahadur, apparently oblivious to the flying snow, staring up at the sky, one ungloved hand pointing upwards.

'There, sir… Up there!' he cried excitedly.

Mallory stared upwards, eyes narrowed to slits. For a moment all he could see was whirling clouds of snow. Then he heard that strange hiss once more, and an instant later it came into view, outlined a stark black against the white of the snow.

'Airplane – no motors,' Bahadur announced.

'A glider,' Mallory corrected him automatically, staring up at the big plane. The only sound it made was caused by the hiss of the wind under its huge wings. It was like no glider Mallory had seen before. It looked big enough to accommodate a couple of armoured personnel carriers, and then some.

As suddenly as it had appeared, the glider had vanished and the strange hissing noise had died away, as if the pilot had finally found the course he was searching for. It was then, as he stared upwards into the whirling white gloom, that Mallory remembered where he had last seen a plane like that.

It had been in an old documentary film, grey and jerky of the D-Day airborne landings of June 6th, 1944, in Normandy. The plane he had just seen was a troop-carrying glider of the kind that no army in the world had built since World War Two.

For what seemed a long while, the two men, one tall and white, the other brown, squat and slant-eyed, stared at each other in a heavy, brooding silence, broken only by the mournful howl of the wind. Then suddenly, Mallory was galvanized into action.

'Sergeant Ross! Sergeant Ross, close up the men!... At the double now! *This is an emergency...*'

3

The glider-pilot streamed with sweat. In the green glow cast by the instrument panel, his young face was contorted with fear and fatigue, the veins standing out at his temples, as he fought desperately to keep the glider airborne.

It was now two hours since the tug had cast them off over the Gulf of Finland and had gone zooming away just out of range of Finnish radar. At ten thousand metres all had been comfortable and easy, and the pilot had busied himself happily with his calculations. On paper, it looked as if he would be making an almost record glide – though naturally, given the secret nature of the mission, the flight would never be listed in the records.

But that had been before they had hit the snowstorms over Central Finland. The wind had struck the frail craft like a blow from a gigantic fist, buffeting it from side to side alarmingly, so that within minutes even the veteran paras of the Red Eagles had been reduced to ashen-faced, vomiting wrecks. Now the young pilot, his arms feeling as if they were being torn from their sockets, battled to guide the frail craft through the white-out while Major Gusiev held on to the back of his seat, watching the whirling white wall of snow in front with ever-growing apprehension. Time and time again, he just managed to restrain himself from asking that overwhelming question: 'Do you think we're going to make it, Sergeant?' But he dared not reveal his own dark forebodings to the young conscript; he knew the fellow was doing his best – and more. He didn't want to add to his worries.

Time passed leadenly. For a while they seemed to be flying on their side at a hair-raising angle, the pilot fighting all out to right the craft, the muscles bulging through the thin material of his jacket as he summoned up every ounce of strength. Shortly afterwards, the plane went into a series of sickening short dives, threatening to go into its final death-glide at any moment, and there were screams of terror from all on board.

It was well after midnight when the glider-pilot finally threw in the sponge. They were down to one thousand metres and losing height rapidly. He didn't know where he was, and the white-out was as bad as ever; there was no prospect of a lull in the snowstorm.

'Comrade Major,' he said miserably, freeing a hand for a fleeting instant and wiping the sweat from his brow, 'I've got to land. The storm might just blow us into a built-up area, and that really would be the end.'

'But haven't you any idea where we might be?' Gusiev asked desperately. He knew all too well that a landing near a town could mean precisely the terrible diplomatic disaster his masters feared.

Grimly the pilot shook his head, holding the bucking glider as it yawed alarmingly to the left.

'*Horoscho!*' Gusiev commanded, knowing that they couldn't go on like this. 'Bring it down as low as you dare. Whenever we spot open country, we land. *Davai!*'

The pilot breathed a sigh of relief. Gusiev made his way as best he could to the rear, where his men sat huddled together, white-faced and groaning. The entire fuselage now stank nauseatingly of vomit.

'Now listen to me, Eagles,' he commanded above the hiss of the wind in the fabric, as the glider swayed alarmingly to port yet again, 'we're going to land soon. When I give the command, you will raise your feet from the floor. Each man will lower his head and shield his face, with his arms clenched so.' He demonstrated. 'Immediately we're down, you will–'

The pilot's excited voice suddenly interrupted his impromptu lecture. 'Comrade Commander! We're going down. I've spotted a place.'

Now the ancient glider's nose tipped downwards sharply. At a forty-five-degree angle it hurtled downwards through the snowstorm, the wind buffeting the wings so that they screamed like a tormented banshee.

Hurriedly, Gusiev and his men took up their positions for landing. Up front, the pilot hunched over his controls, face glowing eerily in the reflected light, craning his body forward, eyes peeled for the first sight of a landing spot. Gusiev swallowed hard and felt a nerve beginning to tic at the side of his dark face. How had soldiers ever been able to fly in these things in the old days? Perhaps men had been braver in the Great Patriotic War. Things had been simpler then. At least you knew who your enemy was in those days. Now, it seemed, the whole damned world conspired against the Soviet Motherland!

Down and down the flimsy plane hurtled. Suddenly it gave a bone-shaking shudder. The pilot dragged the nose of the plane upwards madly until they seemed to be standing on end. Gusiev knew that in fact the youngster had put down the air-brakes and brought up the nose to decrease the glider's speed even further, but it didn't make him feel any more comfortable. Now, soon, the glider would come sweeping in to land – he hoped.

'Feet up, heads covered… Prepare for landing!' Major Gusiev bellowed, and then bent his head into his arms like he had seen old men do back home when they prayed.

Now the glider was racing in at over a hundred kilometres an hour. The snowflakes were pelting the windscreen like vicious flak, so much so that the wipers could barely cope with them. Half-blinded, the young pilot started to bring her down as best he could. Suddenly a sharp, jagged shape loomed out of the flying white. A clump of firs! In the nick of time he forced her to the left. As they rushed by, he could hear the trees tear at the fabric. In a moment the fuselage was flooded with icy air and the roar of a howling wind.

'Land!' There it was, glimpsed through a sudden break in the snowstorm. A field, it looked like – and no obstacles.

'Here we go!' the pilot yelled in a cracked voice, and held onto the controls for dear life. Now he had full flaps down, speed constant and just above stalling speed. It was the classic approach, save for one thing – he could hardly see a damn thing.

Another grove of firs came rearing into view. *Up* the plane rose at the very last moment, and cleared them. Now he was coming down again. Behind him, the Eagles moaned and groaned. This was all so very different from dropping out of a plane at twenty thousand feet!

Suddenly the plane hit the ground with an almighty thump. Two thousand pounds of men and material felt the impact. There was a great rending crash. Wood squealed shrilly in protest. Canvas flew in ribbons everywhere. The barbed wire wrapped round the skids to shorten the landing distance snapped like old string. Sending up a great wake of flying snow, the glider ploughed on. The pilot gasped with horror. A whole damned forest seemed to be barring his way. He jerked at the stick. The glider veered to port. Almost instantly it went into a skid; perhaps there was ice under the snow – he didn't know or care. Now he was fighting for his very life, his breath coming in short, hectic gasps, as if he were in the throes of sexual ecstasy.

On and on the plane careened, its guts being ripped out as it raced across the surface of that great snowfield. The pilot battled her every metre of the way, escaping catastrophe time and time again until, with startling suddenness, the torn and shattered fuselage of the glider reared up into the air, tail first, slamming into some unseen obstacle.

Major Gusiev felt himself being thrown to one side. The canvas tore. Suddenly he was outside, and falling. Next moment he slapped into soft snow and lay there, gasping and winded, as slowly, very slowly, the glider began to descend, bearing with it its cargo of shocked and dead Eagles.

It was hellishly cold. The icy wind raced across the tundra at eighty kilometres an hour. It had stopped snowing at last, but still the wind raised the snow devils into wild dances around the weary feet of the marching men, lashing their crimson, streaming faces with razor-sharp particles of snow. Already icicles had begun to form in their eyebrows and moustaches.

But Major Gusiev, in the lead, allowed no time for rest as he hurried his men across the snowy waste. Thirty minutes before, they had ignited the thermite grenades, and the plane, with its dead Eagles and its young pilot speared through the chest by the stick, had gone up in flames immediately. Now he wanted to be as far away from it as possible, in case anyone came to investigate – though only a crazy man would want to be out on a night like this.

Now, as far as he could judge, he and his remaining ten Eagles were some ten kilometres away from the strait through which the English bandits had to pass – assuming old Bogodan was right. Anxious to be there and under cover by dawn, come what may, Gusiev forced the pace mercilessly, tongue-lashing, threatening, cajoling his young men, many of whom were still in shock from that crash in the middle of nowhere.

Like punchdrunk boxers, weighed down with weapons and equipment, they staggered ever onwards. More than once, Gusiev loaded himself with an extra weapon from one of his Eagles and carried it until the man had recovered some of his strength. But all the time he forced the pace, knowing that in two hours the sun would appear over the mountains to the east and that he *had* to be undercover by then. So, like puny ants, impotent, insignificant, the Eagles trailed across the icy waste, dwarfed into nothing by that awesome landscape.

Five miles away, another group of young men, also overwhelmed by a sense of their own smallness in the face of the majesty and a cruel power of this terrible country, fought their way forward through the white night.

Led by Mallory, Alpha Team zigzagged their way up the steep mountain face. They had abandoned their kayaks, for now they knew that someone would be waiting for them on the river bank ahead. Their pace would be slower overland, but their mobility greater.

Now they scrambled upwards, gasping for breath, avoiding the stretches covered with snow wherever possible, preferring the ice; for they knew from experiences that the snow could hide deep crevasses, folds – and half a dozen dangers.

With their boots squeaking on the ice, bodies bent to take the strain, they plodded ever onwards. In the lead, his head lowered to avoid the full impact of the biting pre-dawn cold, eyebrows white with hoar-frost, Mallory allowed no respite. During their arctic training in Norway they had taken five minutes' rest every hour. Not now. Speed was of the essence. There would be no stopping. Once Rogers had choked, 'Sir, I've got to stop and have a piss... I'm bursting, sir!'

'Piss in yer pants!' had been Sergeant Ross's harsh command, and Rogers had dutifully 'pumped ship'.

One hour before dawn, the silver light of a sickle moon vanished and they found themselves marching in a murky grey darkness.

'Christ,' Ramsbottom cried in exasperation, 'talk about the bloody blind leading the blind!'

Mallory didn't hesitate. 'Bahadur, up here at the double!' Barely out of breath, the wiry Gurkha came up level with him. 'You take left, I take right,' Mallory commanded, 'keep your eyes peeled. All right, move on!'

Now Mallory was no longer cold, in spite of the icy wind which swept the face of the steep incline. His body dripped with the hot sweat of tension. If he or Bahadur made the slightest mistake, they could lead the rest of Alpha to its death. Now they moved at a snail's pace in the murk, testing each new step for dangers.

At one point Mallory blundered into a snow-covered series of icy boulders. For five agonizing minutes they slithered over them,

166

hearts thumping crazily, wild with panic. Twice he and the little Gurkha took their lives into their hands as they jumped over deep clefts in the rock face, praying that the snow or ice on the other side would bear their weight. On the second occasion, Ramsbottom, the heaviest of them, dropped safely on the opposite side and groaned, 'Sir, do yer think yer could get me an immediate transfer to the Army Pay Corps? The urine's already trickling down into me boot!'

Nobody laughed; they hadn't the strength.

Time passed leadenly. The summit was still not visible – nor was the first ugly light of dawn. Fervently Mallory prayed that it would soon be light, so as to ease the intolerable burden of leading his men through this lethal gloom, which threatened sudden death at any moment.

Just before dawn, with the sky tinged a faint, faint pink behind them as they laboured upwards, it happened. Absolutely without warning, the ground beneath Mallory's feet was swept away. The thin layer of snow vanished immediately, and suddenly he was plummeting downwards. He screamed once, the scream echoing shrilly after him, and then he was gone...

Gusiev would have dearly loved to have flung himself down on the snow and lain there. At that moment, the snowy surface looked to him like the softest, warmest bed imaginable. But he knew that there were things to be done before he and his Eagles could rest. Already the sun was beginning to rise in the east. They had to be under cover and out of the icy wind that swept along the strait before it became light.

'Igloos,' he commanded. 'Divide into sections of three and make igloos... *Davoi... Davoi...* Among those pines lining the bank there!'

Wearily, miserably, his Eagles took out their combat knives and, moving like old, old men, began to cut blocks out of the hard-packed snow. Soon they formed them into little snow shelters, cementing the joints with their own urine, which froze stone-hard in this icy air within seconds.

Gusiev watched for a few moments, then walked off to the bank. As an officer, he wasn't expected to labour with his hands. He would squeeze into the hut made by the corporal and his comrades.

Now the sky slowly started to lighten to the east, as if God on high were reluctant to illuminate the remote, forbidding landscape below. Gusiev took stock of his position. To his front ran the straits, leading into the next series of lakes, shimmering silver to the north-west. They were only fifty metres wide at the most. From his position, hidden in the trees, he could easily spot any signs of enemy movement on the water. He nodded, satisfied, and stared to the south-east, the direction from which they would come. Here he could see the glistening snakes of three rivers winding their way through the mountains to left and right, leading into the straits. That gross KGB man, Bogodan, had been right. There was no way the English bandits could avoid the straits in their boats.

Gusiev's face broke into a thin, wintry smile. He was pleased with himself and his Eagles. After the initial set-back of the crash landing, things were under control once more. The English would walk into the trap like flies into a spider's web. Perhaps by this time tomorrow he would be drinking pepper vodka in the Russian embassy at Helsinki, surrounded by admiring young women and envious KGB men – people who could never have done what he and his Eagles had done, and knew it...

He turned and strode back to where his men worked among the snow-heavy firs, his stride firm, new strength coursing through his tough, lean body.

'Operator,' he barked.

'Comrade Major,' the operator cried, dropping a block of snow and seizing his ultra-light, ultra-powerful radio set.

Gusiev waited until the soldier had removed his right glove and raised the lid that covered the morse transmitter. 'Send this,' he commanded finally, as the Eagle pulled out his encoding pad and tensed with his pencil. *'"A" Code, top priority. To God,'* Gusiev grinned at the pun on Colonel Bogodan's name, which had now become his call-sign. *'From Eagle One. Eagles roosting nest. Expecting prey soon.'* Gusiev paused, wondering for a fleeting instant what the NATO decoders at Cheltenham, soon to receive this strange message via their communications satellite over the Arctic Circle, would make of it. *'Will feed to young forthwith. End.'*

As the young radio operator bent his head and began to encode rapidly, Gusiev turned to the south-east, and repeated those last words softly to himself. *'Will feed to young, forthwith...'* Then he chuckled – but there was no mirth in the laugh.

Next to him, the operator shivered, whether from cold or from fear, no one would ever find out; for he would not survive that day.

4

Mallory slammed into the rocky ledge with a tremendous thump. For an instant he almost blacked out with the shock of that awesome impact. Then instinctively he grabbed for support in the icy darkness. His fingers scraped against icy rock. He howled with pain as his nails tore on the sharp stone, but somehow he held on in that freezing tomb, chest heaving, body burning with agony.

'*Sir... Sir... Lieutenant Mallory!*' called a disembodied voice, from far, far away.

Gingerly, Mallory raised his head. Somewhere in that icy cavern there was another human being. Was it possible? Way up above him, a dark shape broke the grey gloom. A head.

'I'm all ... all right,' he croaked, in a voice that he hardly recognized as his own.

'Thank God for that!' It was Sergeant Ross, and for once the tough Scot sounded genuinely concerned. 'Are ye injured, sir?'

'No, I don't think so... Just shaken... Can you see me, Sergeant?'

'No, I canna. But dinna fear, sir... We'll get ye out of there in a couple o' shakes.'

Mallory took a deep breath. He mustn't show the men just how rattled he was. He tried to calm his nerves and speak normally. 'I don't ... think I can get out under my own steam, Sergeant,' he said carefully.

'Dinna fash yerself, sir,' Ross answered, his voice hollow and booming. 'We'll sling our toggles together. I'm hoping they'll reach.'

Mallory gave a gasp of relief and uttered a

silent prayer. 'Give me the wire when you're ready,' he called. 'I'll look out for the rope.'

'Aye, that we will, sir,' Ross said, forcing warmth and confidence into his rasping Gorbals voice.

As he waited, Mallory could feel the cold stealing swiftly up his legs and into the pit of his stomach. He forced himself to be patient, flexing the muscles of his hands and his fingers, but otherwise not daring to move, for the ledge was much smaller than his body. It was a miracle that he had ever managed to land on it, let alone stay there.

'Lowering away, sir,' Ross called from above.

Mallory swallowed hard. This was it. Up top he could visualize them, strung out, each man taking the strain, backs bent, feet apart and wedged in, as the knotted length of toggle ropes began to disappear into the gloom of the hole.

'Ten feet,' Ross called out, judging that half the first toggle had gone over the side. 'Twenty feet!'

Carefully, Mallory reached out his right hand into the void. *Nothing!* Evidently he was much deeper than twenty feet.

'Thirty feet, sir!'

Again Mallory sought for the rope in the icy gloom. In vain. It still hadn't reached him.

'Forty, sir,' Ross sang out. The earlier

confident note had gone from his voice now. 'We've no much more of it left, sir,' he added.

Mallory hadn't the strength to answer.

'Fifty feet, sir!'

Mallory reached out a violently trembling hand and swept it round in the darkness, praying that his bleeding, battered fingers would touch the rough surface of the toggle rope. But he was doomed to disappointment. There was nothing there.

'I can't … can't find it,' he croaked.

Above, there was silence for a moment, and Mallory had the impression that an urgent conference was taking place. Finally Ross called, 'We've cut down our hold, sir… I'm afraid we've only got another five feet left…'

Ross's voice trailed away into silence, and Mallory swallowed hard. He knew it was now or never.

'Play it out, Ross,' he cried back. 'It'll be all right … *now!*'

Alone there in the icy darkness, Mallory waited, knowing that if the rope didn't reach now, it would be the end. Naturally, Ross would insist that the men should try to clamber down and get him, but he would order them not to do so. They hadn't a hope in hell. The sides were slick with ice; they would never get a hold. It would mean allowing them to slide to their deaths – and he wasn't going to have that. If the rope didn't reach, he would order Sergeant Ross to take command and do his best to get them back to civilization and safety. He would be condemned to die here alone at the bottom of the crevasse, his grave already dug for him in advance.

For a moment, he indulged in self-pity. He was only twenty-six, with so much life ahead of him. Why should he be forced to die out here like this, all alone? Then he thought of the kids who had died in battle in the Falklands. It had seemed to him that the transports carrying the infantry for the last attack out there had been filled with callow, down-cheeked kids – teenagers with skin-head haircuts and boastful, silly tattoos. Not one of them had looked a day older than eighteen. They had died bravely – scores of them – and for what? Rotten half-education in a comprehensive; a council slum, a few hours of fleeting pleasure in some sleazy disco; if they were lucky, a furtive grope with some unwashed, half-grown girl in a back alley. There had been no top-hatted Pop for them; no champagne and boating parties by moonlight; no elaborate mess dinners, with the Corps silver sparkling in the candlelight; no expensive birds in Chelsea mews flats... No, he had had a good life. Now he had to be prepared to pay the butcher's bill.

'That's it, sir.' Ross's voice cut into his

thoughts. *'Fifty-five feet!'*

Mallory felt his heart thumping furiously. It was only with a conscious effort of will that he managed to stop his hands trembling. Hardly daring to move, feeling the veins throb electrically at his temples, his breath coming in harsh, hectic gasps, he began to reach out his right hand and search the icy darkness.

His heart missed a beat. For a moment he was completely unable to speak. He felt as if he were being strangled. With both hands, leaning out dangerously, not caring now, he stroked the coarse, hard surface of the rope, as a mother might caress a beloved first child. Then, and only then, did he cry, 'I've got it... *Haul away, Sergeant Ross!'*

Major Gusiev crouched in the icy igloo. He was cold, but not uncomfortable. At least the icy blocks kept out the freezing Arctic wind. And they had eaten – cold grain porridge, dried hard strips of meat, a lump of sugar each, all washed down by a sip of fiery pepper vodka which had brought tears to the eyes of even the toughest of his Eagles. For a while Gusiev's blood had seemed to be ablaze. Outside, he could hear the soft squeak of the sentry's boots on the snow, as he patrolled the bank, waiting for the first boat to come into sight.

Crouched there, the Russian major looked

at the green-glowing dial of his wristwatch yet again. It was a Timex, and he was inordinately proud of it; he had taken it from a dead Afghan. The bandit had probably been in the pay of the CIA; those rats all were. He sniffed at the memory of those murdering, treacherous thugs. The Afghans often slaughtered unsuspecting young Russian conscripts from behind and mutilated them terribly afterwards. They should have gassed or napalmed the lot of them years ago. He frowned. It wouldn't be long now.

'Comrade Commander,' came a soft call from outside.

He rose hurriedly to his feet. It had to be them. Stooped low, he crawled outside into the new day. Already the sky was beginning to change from a dawn grey into the hard, bright blue of a northern morning.

'There, Comrade Commander,' the sentry whispered, pressing Gusiev's arm hard. Gusiev tugged himself free. In the Red Army, familiarity between officers and men, even in élite units such as the Red Eagles, was frowned upon.

To the east, where the middle river flowed towards the straits, a strange object, camouflaged with branches, was floating idly down the centre of the stream – and another was following it perhaps fifty metres behind.

Gusiev caught his breath. It might be a log, but equally, it could well be the bandits.

Hurriedly he brought out his prized mini-binoculars. They were Japanese-made, small enough to hold in the palm of one hand, but tremendously powerful. Once again, they were taken off a dead partisan in the hills beyond Kabul. Sometimes he thought the whole world conspired against Russia, even the Japs. It wasn't fair...

He focused them. The boat, if it *was* a boat, was too well camouflaged with branches for him to make out its shape, even with the aid of the Jap glasses. But there was no mistaking the human figure that came sliding into view in the calibrated circles of glass. Slumped low and obviously very relaxed, for the current was doing the work and the man had no need to paddle, it could be no one else but the English, with the link man floating fifty metres behind. Who else would camouflage his craft like that? Certainly not some damned duck hunter.

Gusiev hesitated no longer. 'Wake the others,' he hissed urgently. 'Prepare for action! *It's them!*'

Sergeant Ross dropped on one knee and raised his right hand to signal 'halt'. Behind him, Alpha Team stopped dead in their tracks. Ross pointed to his shoulder. It meant 'officer up'. Then he formed a 'T' with the palm of his left hand and the fingertips of his right – the signal for 'enemy ahead'.

Mallory broke away from the rest of Alpha Team. At a crouch, he raced forward across the glittering, sparkling snow, to where Ross crouched in the shelter of a snow-heavy fir.

'Where?' he gasped, flinging himself down next to him, his little Polish automatic at the ready.

'Yon bushes at two o'clock, sir,' Ross answered in a tense whisper, not taking his eyes off his front. 'They've fallen for it. They're watching our boats coming over yonder.'

They had indeed. The two camouflaged logs laden with their rucksacks, which they had hoped would look like hunched paddlers, were drifting downriver, right on cue. 'How many of them can you make out, Ross?' he whispered.

'They're in groups of two, sir, at ten-yard intervals, near the snowhouse. Holy Christ, wouldn't they have got a rollicking from the staffs' – he meant the training instructors – 'Back in the old days!'

Mallory nodded. The little Scot was right. The Russian igloos – for he guessed that the men who had set fire to the glider could only be Russians, out to prevent them escaping – were pretty conspicuous. It surprised him a little; he had thought they would have been better at camouflage.

'All right, Ross,' he hissed, keeping his mouth close to the other man's ears, 'you take Rogers and Ramsbottom and come in

178

from the left. I'll take the rifleman and come in from the right.'

'Sure you'll be all right, sir? With yon Gunga Din, I mean?' Ross asked.

Mallory laughed. 'I didn't think you cared, Ross. Sure I'll be all right.'

He turned, and signalled the others to move forward. Noiselessly they obeyed, and a moment later he was briefing them. As he did so, he noticed that each of them constantly checked their weapons, as if to reassure themselves that they weren't going into this unarmed. Finally Mallory was finished, and asked as a matter of routine, 'Questions, anyone?'

There was a moment of hesitation, then Ramsbottom tentatively put up his hand. 'Yes, sir, I've got one.'

'Fire away.'

'Well, sir...' Ramsbottom flushed, almost as if he were embarrassed.

'Come on, mon,' Ross urged angrily, 'we've no got all day. Piss, or get off the pot!'

'Well, sir, once they figure out we've got them by the short and curlies, like, coming in from both flanks, sort of ... what are we gonna do?' Again he hesitated.

'Come on,' Mallory urged. 'Spit it out.'

'What if they surrender, sir? What do we do with the buggers then?'

Mallory frowned. It was a question he hadn't expected, and at this precise moment he didn't really know how to answer it. They had already seen just how ruthless the Russians could be when they had sunk the West German torpedo boat, but could *they* be equally ruthless? Yet what could they do with prisoners? They were hunted men. They could hardly afford to take on any extra burdens. God only knew what other tricks the Russians had up their sleeve.

'Well, Ramsbottom,' he said carefully, 'I think we should worry about that one when we come to it.'

'Aye – huish all yer blether, mon!' Ross snapped angrily. 'Let's get at 'em first, and take it from there.'

Swiftly they divided into two groups, as planned, and began to creep forward through the snow, with Ross in the lead. Behind him, Ramsbottom, the biggest and clumsiest of the Alpha Team, felt his heart beating so loudly that it must give them away to their victims. Please God, don't let them hear me, he prayed. Next moment, guilt washed over him; there he was, about to kill his fellow human beings, and he was asking God to help him do it!

Gurkha Bahadur felt no such scruples. As he slithered ever closer to the dug-in Russians lining the banks, Mallory could hear him intoning some strange ritual of his own, his breath coming in sharp, excited gasps. Puzzled, Mallory turned round for an instant, and saw that Bahadur's dark eyes were sparkling with almost impossible excitement; he had slung his WZ 62 and was clutching his razor-sharp kukri in his tiny hand. By the look on his face he was just raring to use it.

Now they were only twenty yards away from the humps of snow blocks; behind them crouched the Russians observing the straits, as the 'boats' drifted ever closer to their ambush. Mallory halted, and flung a glance to where Ross crouched. The little NCO gave a cocky thumbs-up sign. Mallory forced a smile, but inside his heart was pounding away like a kettledrum. Angrily, he ordered himself to stay cool. He pumped his right arm down rapidly three times, the signal for 'attack in three seconds'. Ross, his face set in a wolfish grin, nodded.

Suddenly they were up and running, whooping like crazy men. The first burst of automatic fire seemed deafening. Spurts of snow erupted violently the length of the nearest igloo. From somewhere a voice yelled '*Stoi?*' A line of slugs pursued Mallory's running feet. A dark, flat Russian face appeared from nowhere as the would-be ambushers turned to face the attack that had been sprung on them. Mallory fired from the hip and a Russian threw up his arms, seeming to rise in the air, then fall heavily on his back, his automatic rifle whirling through space like a drum major's baton.

A Russian threw a grenade at Bahadur. He ducked, and it exploded harmlessly against a fir behind him, in a ball of ugly yellow flame. The Gurkah whooped and dashed forward. The Russian brought up his automatic to ward off that flashing, deadly blade, but Bahadur parried it easily. Next instant his kukri hissed. The Russian gave a high, shrill scream as his severed head tumbled to the snow to stare upwards at the headless torso reclining against the tree.

'Pour it on 'em!' screamed Ross, red face contorted with fury, snapping off quick, professional bursts to left and right. *'Kill... Kill... Kill!'*

Next to him, Rogers stumbled and fell flat on his face in the snow. Next instant, a vicious burst of tracer hissed towards the precise spot where his head would have been. Ross spun round in time to see a dark, saturnine face peeping from behind the nearest igloo. *'Kill my fucking men, will ye?'* he cried, in a paroxysm of blinding rage. He took aim at Gusiev's face.

The tall Georgian major pressed his trigger. There was a light *click*. He had fired a whole magazine at the young English bandit. Desperately he fumbled for another mag. Too late! Ross fired, face set in a dark death's head.

Gusiev's face crumpled into a red horror,

his nose and eyes smashed back into the shattered ruins of his brains. As he began to go down slowly at the knees, his face seemed to drip on to his chest like red molten wax. Suddenly he flopped to the snow, arms outspread as if he had been crucified.

Now the men of Alpha started to wind up the rest of the igloo line. Doubling forward in desperate spurts, bending and firing, they pressed ever forward. A grenade hissed through the air at Mallory. He ducked and fired in the same movement – and missed. Cursing in Nepalese, Bahadur sprinted forward, slugs cutting angry patterns around his flying feet. A Russian screamed in terror, *'Nyet... Nyet!'* flinging away his weapon. Too late. The deadly kukri hissed through the air. The Russian went reeling back, hands clasped to his face, the blood already spurting in a bright scarlet jet through his clenched fingers, to die writhing and heaving in the reddened snow.

Then it happened, just as Ramsbottom had feared. Immediately to Ross's front, two young Russians, their faces distorted with horror, flung down their weapons. *'Tovarisch... Tovarisch!'* they quavered. One was weeping pitifully, the tears streaming down his young open face. 'No shoot... *No shoot!'*

'Fuck ye!' snarled Ross – and pressed his trigger. The automatic chattered wildly at his hip. The first Russian went reeling back

screaming, hands clasped to the bloody ruins of his face.

'And now you, sonny!' Ross screeched.

'No, Sarge! No!' Ramsbottom's pistol flashed upwards and struck the butt of Ross's automatic, sending his burst of fire sailing harmlessly into the sky. And then it was all over, and their first and only prisoner was down on his knees, kissing Ramsbottom's hands fervently, as if he were the Pope in person. Ross, meanwhile, shoulders bent and heaving as if he had run a great race, glowered at Ramsbottom in fury...

'Well,' said Mallory, as the rest of them looted the dead Russians' kit, stuffing food greedily into their mouths and packing the rest away in their rucksacks for the long march to the coast, 'I suppose we could let him go!'

'Idyut – go!' The Russian radio operator, who was called Piotr and who had learned a few words of English in Kabul, repeated the word happily, his bright blue eyes flashing swiftly from face to face.

Ross took another swig at the bottle of vodka he had found in the dead officer's rucksack, his face flushed and angry; then he looked away in disgust.

'Aye, I think we could, sir,' Ramsbottom agreed. 'He's all on his lonesome and he's got a long trek back. Besides–' he placed his hand across his mouth delicately so that the prisoner couldn't hear – 'he might never make it, like. But at least we're giving him a chance, sir, aren't we?'

Mallory nodded a little wearily. The heady elation of the battle had vanished now, leaving him feeling drained and downcast. 'You're right, Ramsbottom. All right, kit him out with what's left. The rest of you, prepare to move out – and this time it's on Shanks's pony.' He indicated the straits which were already glittering brilliantly with ice. 'The kayaks would be more of a nuisance than anything – and it's going to get worse the further north we go.'

Now the men finished their preparations. For once Ross wasn't his usual fussy, busy-body self – instead, he occupied himself moodily with his own kit and his bottle. Ramsbottom, meanwhile, checked out the Russian. Communicating in sign language, he made sure that the Eagles' radio operator had sufficient food in his pack and a knife, just in case; for this morning, for the first time, they had heard the eerie, mournful howl of a wolf in the distance.

Satisfied, Ramsbottom turned to Mallory, who was staring at the first flakes of the new snowfall as they began to drift down and cover the silent shapes of the Russian dead.

'Shall I let his nibs go now, sir?'

'Yes, let him go,' Mallory answered. He

didn't want the lone Russian to see which direction they would take, though he felt he had little to fear from the man. The Russian would be lucky if he made it back at all in this weather.

'Off you go, then,' Ramsbottom said, and gave the Russian a shove. The radio operator hesitated. He mumbled something in his own language, one hand feeling inside his padded jacket, as if his chest hurt. Then finally he staggered off into the ever-thickening snow.

'Form up,' Mallory ordered. 'Sergeant Ross, bring up the rear, please.'

While the men adjusted their rucksacks for comfort, Mallory crunched through the snow to the head of the little column, avoiding looking at the men they had killed. 'Move out,' he commanded, the snow flakes already beginning to lash his face icily.

To the rear, Sergeant Ross shot his commanding officer a black look. The Sassenachs had no fire in their guts, that was their trouble. Letting yon Russki go like that! And that la-di-la officer was the worst o' the lot! He took a final swig of the looted vodka and felt the fire surge down his throat and into his stomach, bringing with it new energy and determination. Suddenly he made up his mind.

Already the rest were beginning to move away into the whirling gloom ahead. They would never miss him, strung out as they were at ten-metre intervals. His hard, wet hand clutched his combat knife; his eyes blazed with drink and fury. Stealthily he slipped to the rear, casting his gaze right and left in the snow, searching for his victim. He had to find him before his absence was discovered and yon fancy officer Mallory started crying stink' fish in that pound-noteish accent of his.

Suddenly he spotted the Russian. He hadn't got far. He was kneeling, bent over something, busily adjusting a square object at his feet. For a moment, Sergeant Ross's mind was so befuddled with drink and his vision so blurred by the ever-increasing snowfall that he couldn't make out what it was. Then he exploded with rage. The Russki bastard was crouching over a radio! He could see the dull silver glint of the aerial. He had concealed the thing in his thick wadded jacket. So that was what he had been touching just before he had left.

'Why you sneaking rotten bastard!' Ross roared, and lurched forward.

The Russian turned in alarm, one hand still holding on to his mike, and saw the knife held in Ross's hand as he lumbered towards him, weighed down by the great rucksack. *'Nyet!'* he cried, but there was no fear in his voice this time. Now he remembered his slaughtered comrades, shot down in cold blood from behind by these English

187

terrorists who had appeared from nowhere. Now he wanted revenge; he wanted them destroyed.

Turning to his transmitter, he pressed the key down hard. It was 'National' – an open circuit. Sooner or later, the man they code-named 'God' would hear that it had been opened somewhere in Finland, and guess that their mission had failed. Suddenly he felt an agonising spasm of pain, and went reeling back. Again and again, Ross's combat knife plunged in and out of his writhing, screaming body until at last, after what seemed an age, he was still.

For a full minute the crimson-faced murderer towered above the lifeless shape spreadeagled in the blood-spattered snow beneath him, sobbing for breath. Then he staggered away, all rage spent, breaking into a ragged trot to catch up with the others, disappearing once more into the raging storm.

Behind, already rapidly stiffening in the terrible cold, the dead man's finger continued to press down on that key. The humming seemed to go on for ever, bearing with it from that remote, icy waste its message of doom...

BOOK FOUR

Home Run

We had survived, and that was our only
 victory.'

A Rumor of War
Philip Caputo

I

'*Nyet... Nyet... Nyet!*'

Colonel Bogodan brought his pudgy fist down so hard on his desk that his beloved pistol lying on top of it trembled like a live thing, and his informant at the other end of the telephone line gasped with shock.

'*Surely it is not possible?*' he gasped. It was more a plea for reassurance than a question.

'I am sorry, comrade Colonel,' replied the signals intelligence officer at the other end. He spoke politely enough, but the shock at Bogodan's outburst was still clearly evident in his educated Muscovite voice. 'But it is so. We have received the same signal from three different points so far, and I can assure you that more might well come in before the hour is out. Kazan reported it, Smolensk too. Even as far as Val–'

'You mean that the Red Eagles' mission has failed?' Bogodan interrupted him miserably.

'I think one can assume that, comrade Colonel,' the signals officer replied, in a prissy, holier-than-thou tone that was beginning to grate on Bogodan's already frayed nerves. 'Otherwise the signal would be in code.

Besides, it is still continuing. As I speak to you, my people are continuing to pick it up. I don't know exactly why. It could be–'

'*Spasibya... Dosvedanya,*' Bogodan cut him short, and slammed down the receiver, rising to stare at himself in the dirty, fly-blown mirror on the wall of his office-cum-bedroom.

What a mess he looked! His face was puffed up with the vodka he had consumed during the night, his red eyes ringed with dark circles. He had been well over his hundred, that was for certain. Why else would he have called a whore in the middle of the night? Of course, he had told the duty militia officer that it was an urgent inquiry of a secret nature and had ordered him to ensure that the call was secure. But it hadn't been that at all. For some reason, his passion – or lack of it – had run away with him. He had asked her terrible things; once he had pleaded with her to let him rip off her pants with his teeth... He shuddered at the memory. What a fool he had made of himself – he, Colonel Boris Bogodan, twice Hero of the Soviet Union, an officer who had been received with honour by every General Secretary since Old Leather Face himself.

Now those brave boys, those young Red Eagles he had waved away so confidently, were dead. He knew it. They were dead. Slowly, a fat tear began to roll down his gross, debauched face. He choked and reached for another bottle of vodka under his desk, still sobbing. Almost unaware of what he was doing, he filled a tumbler with the fiery liquid; took the salt cellar; poured a trickle of salt in the 'V' formed by the skin of his extended forefinger and thumb, licked the salt, cried *'Nastrovya'* – and drained the glass in one gulp.

His blood ran fire. The tears stopped at once. He looked at himself in the mirror and approved of what he saw: a fine-looking, brave, intelligent officer. Admittedly he had certain embarrassing minor problems of a physical nature, but mentally his grip was as firm as ever. Defiantly he stared at his wavering image in the old mirror – a trophy looted many years ago from one of the fine bourgeois houses that had once graced this very street.

He took another sharp pull at the vodka, this time straight from the bottle; he couldn't be bothered to pour himself a glass. His mind was beginning to function again, and he needed the additional fuel.

Naturally, he would be held responsible for the Finnish fiasco. Whatever had happened out there in the land of the blubber-eaters, it would be nobody's fault but his own. No doubt as soon as that pretty-faced Moscow general heard the news, he would be on to him, blaming him, telling everyone he, Bogodan, was responsible. After all, it had been his project. A bunch of élite special troops had been wiped out, there was an international incident in the offing, and the damned laser cannon secret was *still* in enemy hands. *'Boshe moi!'* he cursed. He *had* to stop them before it was too late. But how?

Bogodan sat down suddenly. Outside, Leningrad was coming to life again. There was the rattle of the blue-painted trams, the honk of the ancient taxis fighting their way through the streets crowded with workers, the jingle of bicycle bells. It was a happy sound, and Bogodan always had liked it, for it reminded him of the people who gave him his mandate, the people he had worked and fought for these forty years. Not the Central Committee, not the Party, not the KGB, not even Russia; but the people of Leningrad. Probably most of them had never heard of him – they were too concerned with their televisions, their jobs, their holidays on the Baltic, the remote possibility that in five years' time they might have a car allotted to them. Yet, he knew, the welfare of people like them depended on people like him; for the city was surrounded by enemies – enemies he must smash! Once again, Bogodan, drunk by now and weeping softly, smashed his chubby fist down on the desk in impotent rage. Why were things always going wrong for him, when he had always tried so very, very hard?

His vision blurred, Bogodan stared at the big map of Finland pinned on the wall, concentrating on the area the blubber-eaters called 'Oesterbotten', the coastal area. There, the rivers which ran through the central lakes had their estuaries – at Pietersaari, Kokkola, Raahe, Oulu, and all the rest of those damned outlandish names of theirs. Could it be possible that these English bandits would take the easy way out, cross the Gulf of Bothnia into Sweden, and take the short route to Norway? After all, they had been first discovered at sea in the Gulf of Finland, in canoes. They knew something about sailing, and there must be plenty of small boats along the coast they could steal. 'Give me knowledge,' Bogodan prayed, inadvertently addressing a God he had believed dead, non-existent, these sixty years. 'Knowledge – *please.*'

Or would they take the long route to Norway, through that remote Finnish Territory to the north via Kittila? He sucked his teeth and pondered. But surely they would expect a surprise raid over the border into blubber-eater country? After all the narrow strip of Finnish territory which led to Norway, was fringed by the Soviet Union. No, their most likely route had to be across the Gulf of Bothnia, somewhere between Pietersaari

195

and Oulu.

His mind made up, Bogodan stared drunkenly out of the window, wondering what he could do to stop the bandits now. Outside, the sun was beginning to slant beautifully across the harbour. He remembered those old days, when they had hated that sun for bringing with it the Fritz planes from the sea – heavy, cumbersome flying boats that had come weaving in through the black puffballs of flak, to sow the Sound with mines or launch their tin fish – deadly torpedoes filled with a ton of high explosive, which had put the fear of death into the admirals of their Baltic Fleet and, in the end, forced them to abandon their ships.

'Flying boats – *seaplanes!*' Suddenly he snapped his fingers excitedly. 'Of course!' His indecision forgotten now, he grabbed the phone and barked, 'Flag officer! Flag officer, Oranienbaum Naval Base – quick! I don't care what time it is, man. Naval officers are workers too. Now hurry it up, man. *Davai!*'

Strung out in a long line, they plodded doggedly on through that vast, empty landscape, like the last men left alive on this earth – a trail of insignificant ants across that dazzling-white carpet of hard snow. But though empty, that enormous steppe breathed hostility, awesome and brooding; it was as if nature herself conspired to hinder their progress.

The temperature was well below zero, and the cold was murderous. Time and time again, an icy wind raced across the limitless snowfield, lashing their strained young faces so cruelly that they sobbed with pain.

Yet in the lead, Rifleman Bahadur felt a glow of pride. Hadn't the officer chosen him as the only one who could still march and guide the team through this inhospitable terrain? It was just as his father had said to him, that day when they had trekked from the mountains to the recruiting station at Daiwan so that he could present himself to the big white men; 'Obey your officers, my boy. Show them respect, and one day, sooner or later, they will show you respect in return.'

He knew, of course, that his father must be right; he always was. Had he not served twenty-one years in the Gurkhas himself? Did his kukri not bear the notches of the four Germans he had killed in North Africa and Italy? His father had seen much, done much; he was a man of the world. Yet at first he had had reason to doubt his word. The white men hadn't shown respect. Even these brave men with whom he had the honour to serve now, hadn't really respected him at first. He had felt it in his bones. But now it was different. They respected him – more, they *loved* him, entrusted their lives to him, these giants from the cities. He turned and flung a glance at his new-found comrades: the officer, bent double under his rucksack, his handsome face hard and strained; the youth Rogers, who had enjoyed too many women, when he had had only one, a prostitute in Hong Kong; Ramsbottom, a good man, a countryman like himself, coming from a remote village called Bolton; and then Ross, the smallest and hardest. Ross might well have been one of his own people, yet he had been the last to accept him. Now he, too, loved him. Ross loved him at last, and that knowledge made his heart leap with joy.

So the little man with the happy, slanting eyes led them ever westwards. Their faces shone with ice now, and every breath they took was like the blade of a sharp knife stabbing their lungs. Yet while their upper bodies froze, their legs were ablaze with sheer agony with each fresh step they took. Indeed, it took a superhuman effort of sheer willpower simply to raise one snow-heavy boot, move it yet another half a yard and then repeat the wearisome performance.

Thus they struggled on, making their way as best they could across this cruel, endless landscape. Mallory's compass was hopelessly unreliable now, its readings wildly distorted by their proximity to magnetic north, and it required all Bahadur's native cunning to guide them. He scoured the terrain for green patches of moss on the snow-heavy birches, indicating north; for the line of trees on the horizon bent by the prevailing wind, which always came from the north-east; for the thicker growth among the stunted firs which might mean that they were exposed to a south wind. Occasionally, he would catch a fleeting glimpse of the pale yellow ball of the sun, and make a quick estimate of where west lay by means of his wristwatch. When all else failed, he would stop and sniff the icy air as he had done in his native mountains.

It was on the second day of that terrible march to the sea, when even Ross was almost ready to admit defeat and they had lightened their packs of everything but the remains of their food and fifty rounds of ammo per man, that Bahadur stopped in his tracks and began to howl like a mad dog.

The little column stumbled to a ragged halt, their eyebrows and beards gleaming white with hoarfrost. For a moment they swayed on their feet, unable to understand what the little brown rifleman was shouting about.

Then Mallory had it. He was crying, *'Salt!'* He shook his head, like an utterly weary man coming out of a drugged sleep. What the hell did he mean? Like a drunk, he staggered towards the wildly excited little

Gurkha on legs that felt like rubber.

'What ... what is it, man?' he croaked.

Behind him, the others, their shoulders drooping, arms trailing, stared in open-mouthed stupidity at the two of them, as Mallory slowly reached out a hand to stop the little man shouting.

Rifleman Bahadur obeyed immediately, as he had always been taught; but still the look of excitement remained on his brown face. 'Salt, sir,' he said woodenly, dark eyes inscrutable now, 'I smell salt.' Again he sniffed the air. For a moment he remembered how the animals back home had broken loose and run when they had smelled that delectable tang. In those remote valleys, salt was sometimes as precious as gold itself.

'I don't ... don't understand,' Mallory said in a cracked voice, finding it almost impossible to put the words together into a coherent phrase.

'Salt water, sir,' Badahur replied.

'You mean—'

'Yes, sir, it must be the sea.'

Mallory's exhausted eyes lit up. There was a sudden trembling at the left side of his face. 'You mean, you can smell the sea, Bahadur?' he asked incredulously.

'Yes, sir,' Bahadur replied, his voice matter-of-fact now. 'Perhaps five ... ten miles away...' He held up his gloved fingers to make his meaning quite clear, realizing now just how important his discovery was to these white giants who loved him. 'Over there...'

Mallory followed the direction of his outstretched hand, staring squint-eyed across the glistening surface of the snow-field, as if Paradise itself lay over there. Suddenly he gave a great yell. 'Did you hear that, chaps?' he screamed hysterically. *'Gunga Din here has smelt the sea!'*

2

To their right, a faint, wispy grey against the hard, blue northern sky, rose the smoke of what Mallory knew had to be the small Finnish coastal town of Oulu. Ahead lay the brown smudge of the island of Hailuoto, set against the still, dark-green waters of the Gulf of Bothnia. Beyond lay the unseen coast of Sweden – and safety. For crouching there in the shelter of the snow-heavy birches which lined the shore, Mallory reasoned that the Russians would never dare attack them in Sweden. Their spy subs had caused trouble enough in Swedish waters; they wouldn't want to risk another inter-national incident. Once they were there, they could dump their weapons, march to the nearest railway station with the vital bits and pieces of Fireball and buy themselves tickets to the nearest Norwegian frontier post. From then on, NATO Intelligence would take over. This was, in fact, the home run. But first they had to get across the hundred-mile stretch of the Gulf of Bothnia that lay before them.

At first, Mallory had considered trekking into Oulu with his weary, half-frozen crew, tempted by the delightful prospect of filling his stomach with good food and drink and sampling the pleasures of those celebrated Finnish saunas. Rogers had positively gloated when he had discussed the possibility with Alpha. 'Heck, sir, I'd love that!' he had exclaimed rapturously. 'They run around bollock-arse naked in them places – all starkers – men *and* women, flogging each other with birch twigs. I've seen it in them "X" pictures back in Pompey.'

'Ain't proper, if you ask me,' Ramsbottom had said, frowning. 'I mean, I'm not against a bit of the other, like. But our lass back in Pompey wouldn't like that kind of thing. Showing yer things in public to folks yer don't know!'

In the end, Mallory had rejected the idea, aided by Ross, who had broken his unusual brooding silence of the last couple of days with a curt, 'Wogs, ain't they, sir? Yon Finns, I mean. Probably turn us in to the Russkis as soon as look at us!'

'As I see it chaps,' Mallory said, taking his eyes off the still, green Gulf, 'we can't just walk in there and hire a boat, even if we have got the money in US dollars. No – Sergeant Ross is right. They might betray us – not only to the Russians, who're only fifty miles away as the crow flies, but also to their own authorities.' He looked at their bearded, weary faces and their clothes. 'I mean we don't exactly look like law-abiding citizens, do we?'

Ramsbottom grinned and rubbed a gloved hand across his ragged, dirty yellow beard. 'Aye, and we don't exactly smell like attar of bleeding roses, either, sir.'

'Gots ... randy gots,' Bahadur said in his halting English. 'Smell randy gots.'

'*Goats,* Gunga Din,' Rogers corrected him routinely. 'Mind you, some birds like a bloke to smell a bit high, like. Turns them on, and–'

'Please,' Mallory interrupted him firmly, 'Marine Rogers. Can we not leave your sexual reminiscences for another day? Now there will, of course, be boats up there at Oulu. The place has the look of a fishing port about it. Most of us know a bit about small boats, so we're going–'

'To nick a boat, sir?' Ramsbottom completed the sentence for him. Judging by the frown on his broad Yorkshire face, he didn't

203

quite approve of the idea.

Mallory laughed softly. 'Of course, we'll leave the owner an I.O.U., Corporal. Completely legit and above board, naturally. We'll sign it, even. What about Poole Urban District Council? That'll give the owner something to think about.'

Now it was the others' turn to laugh. Under normal circumstances, the little southern harbour town was their home base, though some of the more left-wing councillors didn't altogether welcome the presence of a special undercover organization in their midst.

'They'll only put the bluidy rates up,' Ross growled. 'Yon Commie buggers!'

Mallory dismissed the subject. 'All right, this is how we're going to do it, chaps...'

It was very dark and very cold. Already the frost was beginning to creep in on all sides, settling on the snow-bound wooden houses like brilliant, sparkling icing, making their timbers creak and groan alarmingly as it tightened its grip. The only light was the faint silver cast by the stars.

For Mallory and his men, now creeping into the outskirts of Oulu, the weather was ideal. All the town's shutters were already battened down for the long, cold night, and nobody in his right mind would venture outside. Those inhabitants who were still awake were probably drinking themselves into insensibility with that fiery *aquavit* of theirs – the only way to relieve the terrible boredom of their lives in this remote northern latitude. He had seen the same thing often enough in Northern Norway during his Arctic training. As for the local fishermen, he guessed they wouldn't be about till first light. He glanced at the green-glowing dial of his watch. Nearly midnight. That gave them, say, five hours before dawn in which to find the right craft, and fuel it for the hundred-mile trip across the Gulf. But by that time, with luck, they would be well on their way.

Now they crunched stealthily over the hard-packed snow, their shoulders wreathed in frost, heading for the humped forms of the fishing boats, which looked like stranded white whales in the pale, wintry light. Even from a distance, Mallory could see that the first line of boats, next to the nets glittering like giant spider webs, were useless. They were similar to the fishermen's cobbles he recalled from the Yorkshire coast: big, heavy, open craft. It would need more muscle-power than they possessed to shift them down to the water, a hundred yards or more away. Besides, they would freeze to death in temperatures like these, once they were out on the open sea.

'Make for the huts,' he whispered. 'Keep an eye peeled for a motor boat or a cabin cruiser, something like that. Doesn't matter how small, we'll squeeze in somehow.'

Like grey ghosts, they crept forward to the silent cabins, most of which were raised on wooden stilts to lift them clear of the water at high tide.

'Ross,' hissed Mallory, 'stand guard. I'll check the boats out myself.'

'Yes, sir,' Ross whispered, and raised his automatic.

'No shooting,' Mallory warned urgently. 'Remember, these are Finns. If anyone makes trouble, nobble him one with your fists.'

'Aye, that I will, sir,' Ross replied dutifully, and slung his automatic once more.

Now Mallory and the rest spread out to inspect the score or so boats drawn up beyond the high-tide mark, testing the hulls, checking whether the plastic-covered heaps next to them contained outboard motors, opening gas tanks and sniffing hard, trying to ascertain how much fuel they contained.

Mallory felt a mounting excitement, plus a certain amount of apprehension. Now they were so close to home, he wanted to be off, safe at sea, away from danger at last. The minute he had handed over Fireball's secrets to the first representative of NATO Intelligence they met in Norway, he planned to take himself and his chaps off to the nearest bar and lay one on. And how! After these last weeks of tension and danger, which had changed their lives in so many ways, they deserved it. He knew *he* did.

'Sir,' Ramsbottom hissed through the velvet darkness, 'this one looks okay.'

Mallory hurried to where Ramsbottom bent over a small craft, perhaps some twenty-odd feet in length, with a gaping hole where the mast should have been.

'Diesel, diesel engines,' Ramsbottom said hastily, using all his strength to unscrew the stiff brass cap of the fuel tank.

'Yes, I can smell it. What's the fuel situation?'

Hurriedly Ramsbottom removed the cap, pulled out his combat knife and poked its blade in until he could feel liquid. 'About half-full's my guess, sir.'

Mallory took a quick look at the size of the tank and made a rapid calculation. 'It'd be a bit of nip-and-tuck, but we'd make it – I think.'

'Famous last words,' Rogers said hollowly.

'Yer'll have my famous last fist in yer kisser in half a mo!' Ramsbottom snapped irritably. 'Well, sir?'

'Yes,' Mallory decided, 'this'll have to do. Come on, chaps, let's take a chance. All right, put your shoulders into it. Off we go for the drink. *Heave!*'

They heaved.

A hundred yards away, Sergeant Ross sat

crouched in the shelter of one of the stilt-legged wooden cabins, his hard gaze working from left and right and back again systematically. Seeing Mallory and the rest of the team hard at work, he gave a grunt of satisfaction. They had obviously found a boat. Now they were shoving it across the hard-packed snow and the shingle beyond to the water. And about time, too. He was sick of this mission.

He thought of the Russian, killed in cold blood. He had no regrets – that treacherous bastard deserved to die. For obviously after they had left him go, he had attempted to betray them. In the freezing darkness, Sergeant Ross bit his lip and looked thoughtful.

Of course, none of the others knew what he had done. Soft Sassenach nellies – they would only have pulled long faces and given him some of that damned mealy-mouthed English crap that they were always trotting out. But what if the Russki bastard had managed to get a signal off before he had croaked him? What then? What if the Russkis were on their trail again, and they were all living in a fool's paradise? Shouldn't he have told Mallory right from the start? It was a doubt that had plagued him for the last two days. In a way, it was a betrayal on his part. He should have–

Suddenly all the worries and doubts which

had been torturing Sergeant Ross these last forty-eight hours fled from his mind. Some-one was coming down the track between the huts to his right! He tensed, every nerve tingling electrically, eyes trying to pierce the gloom. Then he had it. There was no mistaking that soft padding sound.

It was a dog! Christ! he cursed to himself. That was worse than a human being. Men could be nobbled easily enough, but animals – that was something different. While his eyes searched the gloom for the first sight of it, his right hand groped for and found a large rock underneath the hard surface of snow.

Then he saw it. It stopped, and raising its long head, sniffed the air. Ross swallowed hard. It was a great big hairy thing. Even at this distance he could smell the animal stench it gave off, rancid, sexual and stomach-turning.

Now it moved forward and stopped again to let out a low growl. Ears sloping back against its skull, it slipped back on to its haunches.

Ross knew the signs. The brute was going to jump any second. Suddenly he lunged forward, clamping one hand around its long muzzle, cutting off the first bark. He raised the stone. The dog beat him to it. Its paw lashed out savagely, the claws raking across Ross's right cheek. He yelped with pain, and blood splattered the snow.

Holding on grimly, he brought the rock down hard. The animal's agonized howl was stifled as Ross squeezed hard at its muzzle. Now the hound dug in its hindlegs and started to drag him backwards. Once more he brought the stone crashing down and heard it thud against the dog's skull. Still it kept pulling. Now he was slithering through the snow on his knees, fighting hard not to let go of the muzzle, his nostrils sickened by the heavy, rancid animal smell.

'Die, you bastard... *Die!*' Ross grunted, through gritted teeth. With the last of his strength he crashed another tremendous blow on the creature's head.

It trembled convulsively, writhing back and forth, almost slipping from his sweat-soaked grasp. Then suddenly it went limp, weak and pathetic, and lay on its side breathing shallowly, in its death throes.

For what seemed an age, Ross simply slumped there, gripping the animal's muzzle, with the blood still dripping steadily from his lacerated cheek. Finally he roused himself. He slammed the stone down one more time. In the same instant that the dog died, a light suddenly went on in the cabin opposite and a harsh voice cried something in Finnish. Realising his danger, Ross stumbled blindly after the others as if the devil himself were after him.

Seconds later, the engine of the stolen boat gave its first joyful stutter, but by now more and more Finnish civilians were beginning to pour out of the houses into the pre-dawn gloom, shouting and crying in their unintelligible tongue, racing across the crisp, hard surface of the snow to where Ramsbottom laboured over the motor, cursing and sweating, while his comrades watched and waited apprehensively.

The stutter turned into a long, doleful whine. Mallory dug his nails into the palms of his hand until it hurt. The Finns were only fifty yards away now, and some of them were armed. Surely they weren't going to be caught now? The whine grew into a shriek. Next to Mallory, Rogers and Bahadur unslung their automatics and crouched. The shriek was almost ear-splitting now, and the air was filled with the cloying stench of diesel. '*Make it start,*' Mallory prayed. '*For God's sake, make the bloody engine start!*'

Rogers dropped to one knee and took aim. Mallory didn't know what to do. Should he order him to stop? The Finns were almost upon them now. A sudden thunder. The engine burst into life. In the shallows, the still water was thrashed into wild, white fury. The prop was turning! The little boat trembled like a live thing, impatient to be off.

'Fire a quick burst over their heads,

Rogers... Take care now,' cried Mallory.

Rogers didn't need a second invitation. He pressed the trigger. Slugs spurted into the gloom. The civilians skidded to an abrupt stop. Suddenly the air was thick with cries of awe, of rage, of confusion.

Whatever they were, Mallory didn't care. 'All aboard, for Christ's sake!' he yelled, and with all his strength he heaved against the bows. The little boat moved easily. Then he flung himself aboard after the others, landing in a heap in the wet bottom. Within seconds they were chugging out merrily into the Gulf, pursued by the scarlet stabs of flame from ancient shotguns, laughing crazily like jubilant schoolboys released from their lessons...

3

'But I really can't understand why a Soviet citizen should not be allowed to possess a video, comrade Colonel,' the blond navigator complained, as the flying boat droned on and on over the sparkling green of the sea far below, the lights flashing on and off in the radar dome.

'The video itself is not important,' Bogodan lectured the young senior lieutenant routinely, not much interested in the subject. 'It is what will be shown on the apparatus. It is a typical capitalist trick to undermine the loyalties and responsibilities of our citizens. There will be political films, capitalist luxury films, pornography – the usual things to make our people dissatisfied. What cannot be shown on Soviet television should not be available to be seen privately, you under-stand.'

'But I have never seen any pornography,' the navigator said cheekily, 'and I've been in the Red Fleet six years. Before I joined, I always thought that sort of thing was part and parcel of a sailor's life. Red light dis-tricts, wine, women and song...' He grinned easily and shoved his leather flying helmet to the back of his blond head. 'Even the whores in Leningrad are too dear for me, comrade Colonel. We senior lieutenants are not paid too well.'

Bogodan studied the young navigator. The man was impossibly handsome, a real heart-breaker. He thought back to the days in the war when he had been like that too. Then, even mothers of small children had whored for a crust of bread. In that terrible winter, when people in Leningrad had simply keeled over in the streets from starvation and died by the score, nearly every women had been prepared to open her legs in return for something to eat.

God, how powerful and virile he had been then, living as he did on the special rations brought in by motor sledge across Lake Lagoda for the 'Green Caps.' He pressed his pistol hard to give himself reassurance. Now what had he become? A gross, bloated, impotent mess, boasting drunkenly to jailed whores in the middle of the night, threatening impossible acts which he knew he couldn't perform.

Suddenly Bogodan was angry at himself, at the navigator with his cheerful good looks and blond curls, at the whole damned mess in which he now found himself. 'Enough of this rubbish!' he snapped, jowls wobbling threateningly. 'What is our position? What are our chances of spotting these English bandits?'

The navigator's smile vanished at once. Even the humblest member of the Baltic Fleet had heard of Colonel Boris Bogodan and knew it wasn't wise to incur his anger. He stabbed the map spread out in front of him on the little trembling table. 'We're here, comrade, flying due north-east, directly between Finnish and Swedish air-space. Both their radars will have picked us up, naturally, but they can do nothing about it. We are very definitely in neutral territory.'

'That I know. Get on with it.'

'Well, as you know, we picked up the Finnish call from the local radio station at

Oulu, reporting a boat was stolen just before dawn–'

'So we can assume that it was the English bandits who stole it,' Bogodan interrupted the young naval officer. *'Boshe moi,* please don't play the policeman. Leave that to me. All I want to know is when we can expect to spot their boat.'

The navigator flushed and to hide his confusion, bent over his chart and fiddled unnecessarily with his instruments, before announcing, 'At this air speed, and pro- viding the head wind doesn't increase – flying boats are very sensitive craft – we should breach the general area of where the boat should be, estimating its speed at between ten and fifteen knots–'

'Get on with it, man!' Bogodan cried in exasperation. Why was it that every one these days treated him as if he were simple- minded and explained everything at such damned length? *'When?'*

'In about two hours' time, comrade Colonel,' the navigator answered hastily.

'Horoscho.' Bogodan digested this inform- ation for a moment. Meanwhile, the heavy, old-fashioned plane droned steadily on, the two pilots up front routinely searching the horizon from left to right like spectators at a tennis match. Then he once more turned to the navigator.

'Now, once we have spotted them and

correctly identified them as our Englishmen, we must come down to apprehend them. It is important for our authorities to know if these criminals have reported anything to their bosses in London by radio. That is possible, isn't it?'

The navigator sucked his teeth, and Bogodan noted enviously that they were his own, excellent and dazzling-white as well. Most Russian men of his age had already lost their teeth due to their poor diet. 'Well, comrade Colonel, as long as the sea stays the way it is, we can land, naturally. But above wind force seven...' He shook his head. 'Then it becomes dangerous.'

'But this is a seaplane! It is built for landing on the water, surely?'

'Of course, comrade, of course,' the navigator said nervously. 'But it isn't a question of landing, comrade. In a rough sea, we might be unable to take off again – and then we'd really be sunk. What I mean is, comrade,' he added, 'we'd have to make it on the surface all the way to the nearest land...' He shrugged, leaving Bogodan to draw his own conclusions.

Bogodan, however, remained unmoved. He pressed his pistol hard. Things would work out well; they always did for old Boris in the end. Nothing of any real importance could go wrong.

'You worry too much, young fellow,' he

216

declared in a sudden expansive mood. 'The weather seems all right to me. Let's worry about it when the time comes.' He leaned back in his seat and taking out his vodka flask, took a hearty swig before offering it to the blond boy. 'Pop a pull of that beneath your collar,' he said in the style of his youth. 'You were talking earlier about pornography. Well, I'll tell you something I once saw when I was about your age.' His little red eyes sparkled at the old memory. 'There were these two women – one of them a youth leader in the Young Pioneers, by the way. Well, it so happened I was present at their camp when the vodka had been flowing a little too freely, and...'

The problem of video sets forgotten, the navigator leaned forward, intrigued, while behind them to the south, the sky started to darken ominously and a wind began to ruffle the sea, heralding the storm to come.

'Up came a spider, sat down beside her, whipped his old bazooka out and this is what he said...' they bellowed in joyful chorus, as the boat chugged steadily eastwards, bouncing up and down merrily on the green sea, with a steady wind from the east speeding them on their way to safety.

'...*Get hold of this, bash-bash, Get hold of that, bash-bash... I've got a lovely bunch o' coconuts... I've got a lovely bunch o' balls...'*

Mallory, who was singing every bit as lustily as the rest, remembered that time on the plane to London from Ascension Island; how drunkenly happy they had been then! Now that day seemed light years away. How they had changed!

'...*Big one, small ones, balls as big as yer head... Give 'em a twist around yer wrist and fling 'em right over yer head...*'

Ross took the blood-stained handkerchief from his lacerated cheek and nodded to the south. 'Something brewing up there, sir,' he said moodily. So far, Ross was the only one of them not to be infected by the general mood of relief and jubilation, but Mallory knew that the Scots took their pleasures sadly and thought little of it. Momentarily he broke off singing and stared in the direction that Ross had indicated.

To the south, the summer sky had begun to turn a dull, ominous brown, with patches of scudding cloud. The sea, too, was beginning to break white. Even as Mallory stared, he could feel the planks beneath his feet start to vibrate and the little boat begin to yawp. Evidently Ross was right: there was a storm in the offing. Letting the others carry on singing, he nodded to Ross to let him take over the tiller.

Thirty minutes later, the storm hit them with full fury. Immediately, visibility was reduced to nothing. The wind screamed across the white, heaving water, sending the little craft bobbing from side to side like a ball in a shooting gallery. At times she seemed to be standing on her stern, bows pointing upwards to the cruel, leaden sky. Then she would teeter there on the white, whirling crest, hesitate as if she had a mind of her own, and dive shudderingly into the trough beyond, her little screw exposed and uselessly threshing the air.

Inside the boat, all was chaos. Bahadur was helpless; lying prostrate in the bilge, his skinny body trembling and retching miserably all the time, he no longer cared whether he lived or died. The others baled furiously, using empty cans, a large jar, even their hands to toss out the water that came pouring in through the gaps in every plank, each man knowing that the moment the boat became top-heavy, they were finished.

'*Bale, yer buggers!*' Ross screamed crazily, the wind tearing the words from his mouth '*Bale, or we're bluidy done fer!*'

Drenched now, and with spray dripping down his tense face like heavy sweat, Mallory fought the tiller. The sea was a boiling cauldron. One false move, and they were finished – and they had come so far, too. 'Dammit,' he cursed to himself, 'you're not going to get us now!' Exerting all his strength, he held onto the tiller, fighting to ensure that the craft's bows struck straight into the waves. It would only take one of those forty-foot waves to hit them broadside-on and that would be that; they would capsize.

Time passed agonisingly slowly. It seemed to the desperately struggling men that they had never known any other world than this crazy, rolling mass of angry water and furiously howling wind. On and on, Mallory sailed her into those great walls of roaring water. Madly they baled, holding on grimly with one hand, draining water with the other. Up and down they pitched, rearing upwards to the sky to come crashing down forty feet into the slough between two towering awe-inspiring, white-flecked cliffs. It seemed to those five desperate men, alone in that empty expanse of water in the middle of nowhere, that their ordeal would never end.

'Dawn, comrade Colonel.' The navigator gently prodded an ashen-faced Bogodan awake. The flying boat still droned on, the pilots still clicking their heads back and forth like spectators at a tennis match, seemingly unaffected by the wretched night that they, too, must have spent.

Bogodan groaned and opened his eyes narrowly. 'I'm awake already, you fool,' he said with a soft moan. 'You don't think I could sleep in this?'

The navigator forced a grin. 'I think the

worst is just about over, comrade. I have the thermos here. There is soup ... and tea.'

Bogodan held up a pudgy, trembling hand, as if to ward him off. 'Don't mention food to me,' he moaned. 'Give me my flask. It's in my inside pocket. *Please!*' he added with a plaintive note that was unusual for him.

The navigator did as he was asked, and Bogodan took a mighty slug of the raw spirit. Almost at once he could feel the fire coursing through his blood, blasting away the nausea, steadying the violent yawpings of his poor, strained stomach. As a precaution, he took another swig and handed the flask to the navigator.

The latter took a polite sip. 'The captain's compliments, comrade Colonel. He'd like to inform you that he has fuel for two more hours.'

'Good of him,' Bogodan growled, and wiped his paw across his cracked, parched lips, 'but what is that supposed to mean?'

'That in this kind of weather we can search for another couple of hours before we have to turn back. Otherwise, we go down into the drink.' He made a diving gesture with his right hand, like a schoolboy describing a dog-fight.

'You can re-fuel in the air. I have seen it in the cinema many times.'

'But not in weather like this, comrade!' the

navigator protested, aghast. 'It would be suicide. One sudden gust of wind, and with two aircraft so close to one another–' He broke off suddenly. 'It doesn't bear thinking about.' He shuddered violently.

Bogodan, feeling much better now after the pepper vodka, grinned at the apprehensive young man. 'You worry too much, my boy. It comes from having an over-active imagination. Take a tip from an old campaigner. Never worry about what the new day will bring. Consider always the only certainty we know – namely, that one day, sooner or later, all of us, young or old,' – he paused and looked up at the navigator's open, handsome face, aware abruptly of what he was saying – *'will die!'*

Suddenly it was Boris Bogodan's turn to shudder. The huge, lumbering plane flew on, dragging its shadow like an evil raven behind it on the heaving, storm-tossed sea...

Faces haggard and worn, eyes red and sore from peering into the icy wind, muscles screaming out and afire with the strain of steering and baling, the men of Alpha Team battled the dying storm. Thirty minutes ago, their diesel had run out, quickly consumed with the rough usage that the prop had been subjected to it as it had fought to give them headway against the towering, powerful waves. Now they paddled with planks and boards ripped from the bottom of the tiny craft. Even Bahadur, still green with sea-sickness, had been forced into service, labouring bent-backed and breathless against the wind and current.

Mallory's shoulder muscles felt as if they were being ripped apart by red-hot pincers, as he hung grimly to the tiller with the last of his strength. Even so he did his best to encourage the others. 'Keep at it, chaps,' he urged through cracked, salt-chapped lips, eyes red-rimmed and half-closed. 'Keep up the pace... *In... In... Out... Out!* Come on, it won't be much longer now.'

On any other occasion there would have been a surly comment from Sergeant Ross, a muttered, snide remark. But not now. Ross knew that it was only Mallory's strength and sense of dedicated purpose that was keeping them going; the la-di-da Sassenach was showing a toughness that he would never have credited him with. The rest of them were knackered, but the officer gave them no respite, although he was obviously buggered himself. He kept on at them like a terrier worrying a rat.

Now the storm began to ebb rapidly. For a few minutes the wind struck the little craft with one last paroxysm of fury. The boat shuddered from bow to stern. Every timber, every rivet, every plate vibrated with the strain. All around, the water raged in white fury as if it felt cheated of its prey. Then, as dramatically as it had started, the storm finally abated. One moment the wind was howling across the face of the sea at a hundred miles an hour; the next, it had died down to nothing. Suddenly the Gulf of Bothnia was as calm as it had been twenty-four hours before, and the soaked, dazed men of Alpha Team were slumped over their makeshift paddles, sobbing for breath, shoulders heaving.

Mallory thrust the tiller under his right armpit and breathed out hard. At last – at last he needed to fight no more. Now the sea was as calm as the Solent on a warm summer's day. His face cracked into a smile, and he could hear the cake of salt on his features breaking like thawing frost. He had always been told that in the moment of imminent death, one dreamt of one's loved ones back home, or of one's happy days as a youth. He hadn't. All that had kept him going through the last tense, back-breaking hours had been the thought of lying in a soft, warm bed, being fed mountains of fried eggs and toast, washed down with gallons of good, hot coffee, by a pretty young chambermaid, whose skirt had been short and whose plump legs had been clad in sheer silk stockings and high-heeled shoes. So much for romance, he told himself wearily. Obviously he had the soul of a philistine.

Wearily Mallory started to pull himself together. His guess was that they were some twenty miles away from the Swedish coast now, and that the current was taking them roughly in the right direction. At this rate, they might well sight Sweden before noon. By early afternoon they would be within Swedish territorial waters, with a bit of luck, and even if they were picked up by the local coastguard, he couldn't imagine that they would be charged with anything very serious. After all, they were at the mercy of the sea. Perhaps, illegal entry – that would be about it.

'All right, lads,' he called, 'let's get on with it, shall we? We're drifting in the right direction, but I don't think it can do any harm to help Mother Nature out a bit.'

'Bugger Mother Nature!' Ramsbottom croaked, with unusual vehemence for him. 'She nearly buggered *us* back there.' But he picked up his paddle willingly enough and joined the others as they once more began the back-breaking task of propelling the boat to safety.

It was while they were thus occupied that they gradually began to perceive faint noises coming from a southerly direction. At first, they took no notice; they needed all their energy and concentration to keep paddling, moving their limbs like sleepwalkers back and forth. Then slowly, very slowly the droning noise, growing louder now, started to impinge upon their consciousness. One after the other, they rested, leather-lunged and bent over their paddles, turning their heads stiffly in the direction the noise was coming from.

In the distance, a dark shape came lumbering into view, outlined hard and black against the ugly storm-blue of the sky, curving in slow circles, as if it were looking for someone or something.

'Seaplane,' Rogers croaked, and shaded his eyes against the light. 'Can't identify it, sir,' he added, as if the fact were important. 'No type I–'

'*Stoi?*'

Suddenly a vast, inhuman metallic voice echoed and re-echoed across the heavens, magnified a thousand times by the plane's electronics. Although Mallory didn't know what the challenge meant, its impact struck him like a fist in the face.

'Holy cow!' he gasped in awe, as the plane turned to port and he caught the first fleeting glimpse of the bright, blood-red stars underneath its pale-blue wings. 'It's them... *It's the Russians!*'

4

'*Now hear this!*' The booming voice from the air was mannered, unnatural, as if it had been pre-recorded. At any moment Mallory expected to hear a metallic click. '*We know who you are. Please offer no resistance and you will suffer no harm...*'

Mallory looked up as the big old flying-boat zoomed over the boat, its shadow brushing over his upturned face for a moment. Ross sneered, 'Not on yer nelly! Yon Russki buggers'll croak us for sure!'

'Shut up!' Mallory hissed, and waited as the plane roared round in a long, slow curve, his mind racing frantically, wondering what they should do. They were all still armed with their Polish automatics, but what hope did they have of knocking out that flying monster? He had already seen the missiles attached to the underside of the seaplane's wings.

Once more the plane came zooming in, all four engines throttled back so that it could pass as slowly as possible over the bobbing little boat with its helpless human cargo. Once more that monstrous, inhuman voice boomed. '*Hear this. You will throw away what-*

ever weapons you possess... A bosun's chair will be lowered... You will be raised one by one... At the first sign of disobedience...'

The gigantic voice broke off abruptly. In the very same instant that Ross sprang to his feet, cursing obscenely, WZ 62 raised, a brazen light flared beneath the big flying boat's rump. A whoosh. A shower of fiery sparks. With a roar like an express train hurtling along the track flat out, a great, glowing missile shot towards them. Ross ducked instinctively as it flashed right across the boat and plunged into the sea beyond like a red-hot poker being thrust into a bucket of ice-cold water. Smoke rose fast and furious, and as the plane curved again, the awed listeners just caught the last words.

'...We will destroy you!'

On and on that omnipotent voice droned, like that of some harsh, unyielding Hebrew God commanding his fearful, puny subjects to obey him – or else.

Mallory let his shoulders slump as if in defeat, as the flying boat soared away again.

'I dinna care!' Ross cried above the roar of its engines, 'I'll fix the bastard the next time he comes by!'

Sadly Mallory shook his head, well aware that his every move now was being observed from the plane through binoculars. 'I'm afraid that's not on, Ross,' he said, and then, lowering his voice swiftly, as if afraid of being heard, 'All of you make a show of throwing your weapons overboard when the plane buzzes us again.'

'But sir,' Bahadur began to protest, *'Must have bottle!'*

'Shut up, Rifleman!' Mallory hissed. 'I've got a plan. Now here they come again. Do as you are told!'

Yet again the flying boat came roaring in, this time at almost wave-top height, its props thrashing the water into wild fury.

'Throw away your weapons – now!' the inhuman voice thundered.

Mallory gave a shrug as if all were lost and he had no alternative but to do as he was commanded; unslung his own WZ 62 and, holding it high for the unknown observers to see, tossed it into the waves. One by one the others did the same, save Ross, who only obeyed when Mallory raised his fist to him in what he thought himself was a very un-British and melodramatic manner.

But obviously it pleased the Russians, for the next moment the metallic voice rang out again. *'Good. You are wise… Now I shall circle once more slowly and lower the bosun's chair. Your senior man – an officer, perhaps, or NCO – will come up first. Is that clear?'*

Woodenly Mallory nodded his head, while the others stared at him, shocked. What had gotten into him? Why was he giving in so damned tamely?

Mallory waited until the plane had zoomed away once more, before suddenly and to everyone's surprise, embracing Ross as if he might never see him again. Surreptitiously, however, his right hand slid swiftly into the little noncom's pocket to grab what he knew lay there.

'Listen,' he said swiftly, 'if anything happens to me, you're in charge, Ross... Do you hear that, you others? And don't bother about me. Off you go to Sweden, double-quick. You *must* get Fireball back to the UK, come what may.'

'But sir,' Ramsbottom protested, his broad, honest face revealing his bewilderment all too clearly. 'What are you gonna do, sir?'

'No time to explain,' Mallory snapped curtly. *'Here they come again!'*

Now the flying boat was coming in, speed reduced almost to stalling, the crewmen, dark shapes strapped to the side of the plane, already beginning to play out a length of stout nylon rope at the end of which was a little wooden seat. In a moment they would be directly above the wildly tossing boat, and Mallory knew he would have to grab it.

'Now!' the voice commanded.

Mallory rose with difficulty, balancing as best he could on the rocking deck, arms outstretched.

'For God's sake, sir,' Ross breathed, 'watch yerself ... whatever ye're gonna do, sir.'

'I will,' Mallory gasped, and grabbing the rope, swung himself into the seat with the ease of a practiced rope-climber. Next moment the plane was bearing him away at a hundred miles an hour and the little Finnish boat was disappearing below at a tremendous rate.

As the flying boat curved to port, the crewmen began to winch up Mallory, who was sitting in the little chair in a strangely hunched position, hands clutched to his chest as if he were racked with some un-bearable pain.

'*Davai*,' the bigger of the two helmeted crewmen called, '*davai!*'

As Mallory was hoisted up, he found himself staring at floor-level inside the flying boat. To his left, seen through the spread legs of the bigger of the two crewmen, he could see a gross old man in uniform, his chest laden with orders and medals, stand-ing next to a slim, blond youth in flying overalls. To his right, one pilot was crouched over the green-glowing controls, and next to him sat another man, perhaps the co-pilot, handling the mike with which he had spoken to them down below.

Mallory hesitated, as if he were bewildered and didn't know quite what to do next. The man with the mike spoke into it and the interior of the aircraft boomed with his voice. *'Hurry! Get inside! We're going in again!'*

The fat, bemedalled Russian threw his pudgy hands over his ears as if he were deafened by the noise, and the blond youth grinned. But the grin changed swiftly, first to bewilderment and then to horror, as the Englishman clinging there to the bottom of the aircraft, the wind whipping his clothes about him and ruffling his hair wildly, threw up his hands to reveal what he held there.

'Nyet,' cried the navigator in terror. *'Nyet!'*

'Boshe moi!' Bogodan gasped, and fumbled madly for his precious pistol.

But it was too late. The metal, stick-like object was already sailing through the air towards him, its companion hurtling towards the two bemused pilots, trailing behind it a shower of vicious, white incandescent sparks.

In the very same instant, Mallory let go and went sailing down to the sea far below. Above him, the two thermite grenades exploded in a great searing *whoosh*. A huge, all-consuming blowtorch of flame shot the length of the plane. Frantic with terror, Bogodan threw his hands in front of his face, while the navigator fell to the floor, screaming hysterically, rolling madly back and forth, trying to stamp out the blue greedy flames. To no avail. Already both his hands were alight, the deadly white burning pellets imbedded deep in his fat. He sank slowly, his nostrils already assailed by the sweet, cloying smell of burning flesh, hardly aware that he was screaming like a stuck pig, while the flying boat's nose tilted abruptly and it began to race down into its last dive.

'My pistol! If I could only have my pistol!' Bogodan ranted, kneeling there on the steeply sloping deck with the flames racing up all around him, his ears full of the roar of the engines as they raced to their doom. *'God, please... Pistol...'*

At four hundred miles an hour, the flying boat slammed into the water. Its nose crumpled under tremendous impact and immediately it disintegrated. Savage and scarlet, a sheet of flame shot into the grey sky. Wildly, like shrapnel from an exploding shell, shards of metal peppered the heavens with black puffballs. For one long moment, the sea churned and thrashed, hissing viciously, as if it were boiling. Then the plane was gone, as if it had never even existed, with nothing to mark its passing save a single leather flying helmet bobbing up and down gently on the ripples, a strand of bright yellow hair peeping out from it, above the charred, shrunken horror which had once been the navigator's head...

ENVOI

Down below in the harbour, the bells were pealing a joyous welcome. Ships' sirens shrilled, and very faintly they could hear through the open french windows the cheers of the excited, tumultuous crowd as they welcomed home the *SS Canberra*.

Rogers had complained bitterly when Mallory had informed Alpha Team that the Captain-Commandant had ordered them to this remote country house beyond Pompey on the day of the *Canberra's* return.

'Topless they'll be, all them birds. Yer can bet yer last fifty p. They'll be ripping off their jumpers and flashing their tits at them matelots – and we'll be sodding well missing it. Better'n Benidorm beach, it'll be down there!'

But now his regrets were forgotten, as the five of them, smartly clad in their best battle-dress, stood there uneasily in the dark hall. From the inner room came the rattle of cutlery, the clink of glasses, and the occasional bust of hearty VIP laughter: rich, unrestrained, full of its own importance.

Mallory checked his men out for the umpteenth time, wondering who this mysterious VIP was who had asked to see Alpha Team so urgently. Could it be the Queen, or Prince Philip? It had to be somebody pretty important. The Captain-Commandant had even cancelled Mallory's appointment for treatment at Hasler – in spite of the fact that he had still not recovered the full use of his right arm after that tremendous fall from the Russian plane into the Gulf of Bothnia. And the Captain-Commandant, Royal Marines, wasn't noted for being impressed by rank or title.

Down below, the bells continued to toll to celebrate the arrival of the victorious cruise ship, and for a few moments Mallory forgot his bewilderment. Instead he felt a sensation of pride and kinship. For his little team there could be no official welcome like the one being given below; the men of the SBS would always have to slink in and out of the country like thieves in the night. The very nature of their job made that necessary. Yet he experienced a sense of oneness with them in their achievement and their pride in it. For the first time since he could remember, the bitter class-struggle that had nearly ruined Britain in the past had been forgotten and the ordinary people of the country had felt united in common cause with their young soldiers. Out there in the snows of the Falklands, there had been no petty jealousy, envy or class-conflict; nor had there been in the wilds of Finland.

For a little while perhaps, the nation had forgotten its differences and had been animated by the driving force of national pride and purpose. It was a heady feeling. In spite of the dull, throbbing pain in his right arm, Mallory smiled proudly at his men standing there awkwardly and nervously in the gloom of the big hall. Each of them was so different in origin and attitude, yet all of them had been ready to give their lives for an objective about which the world, their country, would never know. For already 'Mission Fireball' had become part of that secret history of the great, undeclared war between East and West which had been waged for decades now.

Suddenly the great double door facing the men of Alpha Team started to open from within. The Brass, flushed with good wine and food, began to emerge; generals and admirals, local civic dignitaries in chains of office, ministers and officials in black jackets and striped trousers.

But it wasn't the Brass, with their giant cigars, who caught the attention of the open-mouthed, gawping Alpha Team. It was the person standing in their midst – the person who had summoned them to this place on the day of victory.

There was no mistaking her in her old-style hairdo and conservative clothes, with her handbag held protectively underneath her arm. And there was no mistaking that hard, incisive voice as she welcomed home the men of Alpha Team and expressed her gratitude for all they had achieved.

Five minutes later they were ushered outside once more, to where the truck was waiting to take them back to Poole. From the harbour they could still hear the bells ringing out in celebration. In a kind of a daze, they crunched across the crisp gravel under the hot September sun and clambered wordlessly over the tail-gate and into the interior. Up in the cab, the driver hurriedly thrust home first gear. He wanted to be away before the staff cars set off down for Pompey.

With a ragged lurch, the truck jolted forward, shaking them out of their trance. It was only then that Rifleman Bahadur, his dark eyes gleaming, broke their dazed silence.

'Hell bell!' he said excitedly. 'That lady, she something... Need in Alpha... She sure got ... *lot a bottle!*'

The others gaped at him in astonishment. They had never heard the slant-eyed little man say so much in all the months they had spent together.

Mallory laughed out loud at the expressions on all their faces, and cried above the roar of the truck's motor, 'But what *would*

Denis say, chaps?'

Even dour-faced Sergeant Ross started to laugh, and soon they were all roaring like crazy men as they wound their way down the sun-dappled narrow English lanes – young men enjoying their time out of a secret war, but destined before long to be embraced by its lethal tentacles yet again.

Team Alpha, the Special Boat Service, was on its way once more...

The publishers hope that this book has given you enjoyable reading. Large Print Books are especially designed to be as easy to see and hold as possible. If you wish a complete list of our books please ask at your local library or write directly to:

Dales Large Print Books
Magna House, Long Preston,
Skipton, North Yorkshire.
BD23 4ND